I0761103

I AM THE GHOST HERE

THE DIAL PRESS
NEW YORK

I AM THE GHOST HERE

STORIES

KIM SAMEK

The Dial Press
An imprint of Random House
A division of Penguin Random House LLC
1745 Broadway, New York, NY 10019
randomhousebooks.com
penguinrandomhouse.com

Some of the stories in this collection were originally published in *Catapult, Ecotone 33, Guernica, North American Review, The Threepenny Review,* and *Zyzzyva.*

Hardcover ISBN 979-8-217-15357-2
Ebook ISBN 979-8-217-15359-6

Printed in the United States of America

1st Printing

First Edition

BOOK TEAM: Production editor: Luke Epplin • Managing editor: Rebecca Berlant • Production manager: Samuel Wetzler • Copy editor: Kathy Lord • Proofreaders: Liz Carbonell, Megha Jain, Taylor McGowan

Book design by Elizabeth A. D. Eno

The authorized representative in the EU for product safety and compliance is Penguin Random House Ireland, Morrison Chambers, 32 Nassau Street, Dublin D02 YH68, Ireland.
https://eu-contact.penguin.ie.

To Josh and Isidore

CONTENTS

I AM THE GHOST HERE

I AM THE GHOST HERE

It is not until my older brother is thirty-three that I learn he's controlled by a puppeteer. The truth comes out after a family emergency, when Jeff is unable to summon the puppeteer on short notice and must appear as himself for the first time. I don't immediately recognize my brother as he hurries through the automatic doors of the hospital. He's usually an alpha male, a tech founder who takes big strides and has a deep, booming voice, but this man is nervous, twitchy, weird.

Normally my brother greets me with a compliment about my appearance. "Looking good, SunnyD," he'd say. "Really fit. You've made some gains?" He nicknamed me for the drink I chugged after judo practice as a kid. I am no longer a jock, but the nickname stuck. This man doesn't use my nickname. He doesn't greet me at all. He slinks up to me with his head down, like I am unfamiliar, except *he* is the one who is unfamiliar.

"Is Dad okay?" he asks, sitting down next to me not far from the triage window.

"I don't know," I reply. "I'm waiting for an update. Mom's in the back with him. We should know something in a few hours. Are you okay?"

"Fine, fine," he says brusquely.

I ask my brother what is going on, why he is so unfriendly. He says that now is not the best time to get into it, that we should focus on my father's surgery and forget about how weird he is acting. He slumps over in his seat as we wait for news. The hospital is noisy with other emergencies. I hear what sounds like a seizure. I hear the aftermath of surgery, screaming that sounds naked in its timbre. I thought a hospital would have better walls. I hope my father will not be screaming like that when he wakes up from his surgery.

"Remember when Dad accidentally ate one of your magic mushrooms and thought he went to Jupiter?" I ask Jeff, attempting to conjure a happier mood. My mother had found these mushrooms in Jeff's backpack and put them into a salad.

"The only time I saw Dad relaxed," Jeff says, nodding. "Maybe if he'd tried a few more shrooms, he wouldn't have had a heart attack."

A few hours later, the doctor emerges. My father has survived the operation and is expected to make a full recovery.

* * *

A FEW WEEKS LATER, my mother holds a family dinner to celebrate my father's return to health. She prepares stir-fried rice noodles, papaya salad, chicken wings, and sticky rice. My brother decides this is the moment to introduce us to his puppeteer. He arrives as the brother we are familiar with, but after a few minutes of chitchat, a petite redheaded woman pops out from inside him and stands by his side. Her name is Michelle, she is Canadian, she is thirty-six, and she has over fifteen years of puppeteering experience. She says she has been scripting Jeff's dialogue since he was in college. I didn't become close to my brother until after he left for Stanford. In the summer breaks, when he returned home, he seemed happier, interested in connection. I'd assumed he had simply grown up, that the time away from home had been good for him.

I can tell my parents are uneasy with Michelle. They've heard rumors of celebrities hiring puppeteers, but no one we know has mentioned using one. Using a puppeteer is not the kind of thing a well-adjusted person should do. My parents don't have to speak to make their opinions clear. As they take turns making faces at Michelle, I ask her polite questions, like how she ended up in puppeteering. She tells us that she is an empath and being other people comes naturally to her. She says that she always wanted to work in the arts, that puppeteering uses her writing and acting skills. She even tells us a long, boring story about her high school theater days. My brother and I nod along politely.

As Michelle talks, it becomes clear that tonight's intro

was her idea, not Jeff's. She says she's grown tired of doing her work anonymously. Unfortunately, no one is interested in offering the praise she seeks. We are preoccupied with noticing how my brother is diminished without her. He isn't gregarious, his arms are crossed, and his lips are arranged in the same permanent frown that he wore through high school, back when he would take his dinner to his room and eat alone while blasting Jane's Addiction.

I try to imagine the kind of relationship I would have with this unmanned brother who quietly broods over his noodles. This guy doesn't seem capable of organizing pickleball games. Instead of accompanying him to concerts, I would see him only at holidays. I refill Jeff's whiskey glass, but the alcohol does nothing to lubricate him. As he sits hunched over in his chair, I hold out hope that the brother I love is somewhere in there. My mother is wearing a sweater that features a panda bear made of Swarovski crystals. Michelle leans over to inspect her face in the crystals, as Jeff would. She pretends to pick food out of her teeth.

"Where do you get a sweater like that, anyway?" she asks. "Do you have to insure it?"

My mother only glares.

I know what Michelle is doing. She is showing off her ability to embody Jeff. She doesn't care that we are upset. I tell her to read the room, but she won't stop doing her Jeff bit. After another fifteen minutes, my mother has apparently held in her feelings as long as she can, and now she erupts. She is a small woman, just four-foot-ten, but the anger makes her tall. My father leans back as she leaps out of her chair.

"This is sick," she shouts at Jeff. "This woman is a stranger! You let a stranger control you?"

"Let's give her a chance," I say. "He's done well with Michelle. Look at what he's accomplished!"

I don't understand why my brother has chosen to be controlled, but after he went to college, he became a good older brother, more like a father or uncle at times. I think back to his holiday visits home when, during my parents' explosive fights, he did his best to reassure me. He said their mutual dysfunction had created two puzzle pieces that could never fit with anyone else.

"It's counterintuitive," he told me. "When they say they want a divorce, what they actually mean is that they want to remain fighting with each other forever. If they really wanted to leave each other, they would have by now." I would have run away from home if not for his assured tone.

"What if this lady drives you to murder someone?" my mother asks. "Only a weirdo would do this job."

"You can trust Michelle," he replies. "I checked her references."

"Michelle seems like a trustworthy person," I say, even though I don't know if that's true.

My mother is upset I am siding with my brother. She stomps out of the dining room, flinging her chicken bones at Michelle on her way out. My father follows, with a look that says, *See what you've done?* Michelle picks the bones out of her lap. My brother looks distraught.

"This was a mistake," he says.

"Give them time," I reply, even though I know time won't help.

Michelle doesn't bother popping back into him now that

the evening is ruined. She leads Jeff out with her hand pressed against his back like she is still guiding him, even from outside. A few days later, I text my brother to ask if he wants to play darts. He doesn't reply. The next weekend, he misses our standing NBA Jam date at the arcade. I eat my mother's pad woon sen noodles alone in my bedroom. Jeff doesn't contact my parents. As weeks pass, he sees me only sparingly. I ask him about Michelle, but my questions disappoint him. He says I remind him of our parents, that I have absorbed their views. He is mad that I didn't leave them. I lived at home during college and have only recently moved a few blocks down the road, close enough to make my mother happy but far enough that I can shut the door on them when needed.

The holidays are triggering for my parents. They stir up secret memories from their childhoods. Ghosts of angry relatives fly around during these fights. My mother's mother is the one who haunts us the most. She'd once said it was a mistake for my mother to move to America. She said my mother was no longer Thai because she left. My mother is racked with guilt even though her mother is dead.

Usually, Jeff would make the situation better with his cheerful stories, his jokes about his bad Tinder dates—though I guess these were Michelle's jokes. But he isn't around to help this time, and his absence adds a new layer of sadness. This year, my parents make a colorful shitstorm. They cry through Thanksgiving dinner, then break dishes on Christmas. My mother threatens to rip out her hair, and my father stands clothed in a bathtub full of water in an attempt to show us he is drowning. My mother threatens to leave my father and move back to Thailand, though she didn't like her life there to begin with. "You think I liked squatting to go tinkle?" she once asked me. Her alcoholic mother had made her life there hell, but still, she always threatens to move back when the days in Washington get too short.

I can't make it through the holidays without my brother. He could talk my father out of the tub. He could make my mother giggle.

"Can't you apologize to Jeff?" I beg my father. "Let him know you approve of Michelle?"

"I don't approve," my father says from the tub, shivering.

"But he came when you were in the hospital," I say. "He was there for you."

"All this time, we never knew who he was," my mother says. "I can't get past that. Did you see how he moped through dinner? No personality. He isn't funny anymore. And Michelle's not Thai. What does she know about a Thai person? Has she ever made sticky rice? Does she make bone broth and smash garlic with her fists? No wonder he's so American. No wonder he stopped speaking Thai."

"Shouldn't have sent him away," my father shouts, as he scoops up tub water and tosses it toward us. "Go to college, get weird ideas for two hundred K."

"What would it take to restore your trust?" I ask.

My mother gives the question some thought.

"An apology would be a start," she says finally. "From him," she adds. "Not *Michelle*."

A few days later, I get dinner with my brother. He is his best self, complimenting my new hat. I tell him I melted it myself, out of vinyl records. I hate being caught between my brother and my parents, but I do my best to negotiate with Jeff and fix the family rift.

"Could you apologize to Mom?" I ask. "It's not your fault she was rude, but you did mislead her."

"This sounds like victim-blaming," he replies. "I haven't done anything wrong. *They're* the ones who should apologize."

Pressing the issue has upset him. His cheeks are red and his forehead is damp. I quickly reassure him that I am on his side, that I have always been. We switch topics to inconsequential nonsense: the Seahawks' offensive line; our weekend plans. Then Michelle steps out and lets us know she is double-booked and will need to leave a few minutes early. I breathe a sigh of relief even though this means she will be leaving me with a version of Jeff I barely know. Even though she is Jeff, she feels like an intruder. We wait for her to make her way out of earshot before we continue the conversation. She lights up a cigarette as soon as she is outside the double doors, then glances down at her phone. I don't believe that I will ever like Michelle, even though I love who she is when she is my brother. I want to accept the arrangement, but I am still having trouble processing the fact that the person I rely on is not him.

"I know this is weird," Jeff says in a low, shaky voice. "Michelle can come off as . . ."

"Grating?" I suggest. "Attention-seeking?"

He shrugs.

"The thing is, I need her," he says. "She saved my life."

He tells me that he had a hard time in college. He was

crippled with anxiety, overcome with self-hatred after failing a test. He was used to being the best in high school, but at Stanford he was surrounded by students who were much smarter than him. He feared going home to our parents, who expected him to graduate at the top of his class. He tried shrooms to ease his depression. A therapist recommended that Jeff hire a puppeteer to guide him. Only the wealthiest kids had access to puppeteers, but Michelle was just starting out and offered to intern for free to get experience. It was only meant to be a short-term solution for his mental-health crisis, but once Michelle took over, the arrangement worked so well that he was afraid to end it. With Michelle inside, he quickly transformed from depressed burnout to successful entrepreneur, someone who didn't hate himself, someone who could pay off his parents' mortgage, someone his family could be proud of. My mother had told him it was the responsibility of the firstborn Asian son to be this person, and now he was. As he talks, I recognize how much pressure my parents put on him. He was meant to be the star of the family. They didn't move to America to produce someone like me. I work as a receptionist in a salon for old rich Asian ladies and have never met a man who was interested in me. Nobody notices me.

Jeff tells me not to blame them for pushing him. He says he is better off now. He enjoys being popular. He enjoys having the confidence to lead a TED Talk, even if Michelle is supplying the confidence.

"But what happens when Michelle leaves for the day?" I ask. "Where do you start and where does she end?"

"There is no Jeff without Michelle," he says. There's some

truth to what he is saying. Michelle is responsible for everything we love about him.

"But, Jeff—you'd still be a person if she quit," I say. "Wouldn't you?"

"I would be a ghost," he says mysteriously. His tone worries me.

After that night, he stops taking my calls. My question must have offended him. I am forced to carry on alone during dinners with my parents, who berate me for failing to land a rich man. Seahawks games are boring without Jeff's amusing commentary. I no longer get invited to parties. I try going to concerts alone, but I feel like an impostor and end up hanging out by myself on the back wall for a few songs before I sneak out.

A FEW YEARS LATER, I see Jeff at the grocery store. My brother is beaming the most a person can possibly beam. He is with someone who I presume is his wife. She clutches his arm and wears a sapphire ring. She is beautiful, even though all of her features are slightly off-center and her legs are the length of her arms. Jeff is in full puppetee mode. I recognize his huge grin as one that's engineered by Michelle. I wave and call out to him. He rushes away, and I realize he is afraid that I will blow his cover. His square wife has no idea that Jeff's charm isn't real.

Later, at dinner, my mother complains that I am sad like her mother—she couldn't have imagined a worse fate than to give birth to the person she was trying to escape.

I protest that I'm not an alcoholic. Am I sad? Yes, probably. But Jeff might be the saddest one of all of us. And I realize then that the reason we dislike the real Jeff is because he is one of us.

ONE DAY, I GET a call from Jeff's wife. She says she found my number in his address book. She tells me Jeff has run off and left her alone with their five-year-old son, Danny. He didn't tell her where he was going. He left in the middle of the night with only one suitcase. She wants to know if Jeff is seeing someone else. I figure Michelle can give us answers. It isn't difficult to track her down—she has a robust web presence. When I call, she tells me she stopped working with Jeff a few weeks ago. She says she has no idea where he is. I look for my brother in our old haunts—music venues like Neumos and the Crocodile—but I can't find him. The police open a case, but a runaway father is not their priority. They assume he has left of his own volition.

THERE IS ONE SILVER lining. After being shut out of Jeff's life, I become a full-time aunt to his son, who looks just like him. Danny is warm, gregarious, and confident. Even at five, he greets me with a compliment when I meet him for the first time.

"My favorite aunt!" he exclaims as I walk up. I am his only aunt.

"My favorite sister!" Jeff used to exclaim when he came home from college.

Danny is eager to hear stories about his father. I tell him the first one that comes to mind.

"One time I caught him swinging a baseball bat at a beehive in our parents' backyard," I say. "He thought he was being heroic, but the bees swarmed his head. He was lucky he ended up with only two stings. My mother told him he was nuts, but she was secretly pleased he had managed to whack the beehive into a neighbor's yard. For the next year, all we heard about was how Jeff outran thousands of bees to save her. 'Stronger than nature' is how she put it."

When Danny is older, we spend our afternoons listening to Jeff's records. I take him to the Sea and Cake concert. He jerks his shoulder to the music just like his father did. He makes me mixtapes.

When Danny drops out of Stanford to start a virtual-reality company, I buy him a congratulatory beer, forgetting he is only eighteen. He is ambitious, like Jeff, but success comes more easily to him. He doesn't have to work hard to be charismatic. He is not the child of immigrants. There is no pressure on him.

Danny is working on a device that allows a person to relive their favorite moments. He says he wants to reunite people with their loved ones. On my birthday, he gives me a headset.

"I know how much you miss my dad," he says. "Now you can spend time with him again."

The machine sends me back to a time when Jeff was home from college for winter break. In retrospect, I realize it was the first time I saw Michelle's version of him. He somberly sweeps up the broken forks and bent spoons, my parents' angry shrapnel, and ushers me away from the house. We head to the arcade and he tells me that everything is going to be okay, that I will be off to college soon and won't have to deal with our parents' fights. He says that his life is much better now. He has wounds from our childhood, but they are not at the forefront of his mind anymore. We spend the evening at a Murder City Devils show on Capitol Hill.

I take off the headset, and Danny is smiling back at me with the same reassuring grin. He asks me if I enjoyed the show and squints at me like Jeff did. That's when I realize why I haven't been able to find my brother. He is inside Danny, pulling the strings.

EGG MOTHER

At thirty-six I turn into a scrambled egg. It happens a few months after I give birth. I am sitting on the patio, nursing the baby, when my feet get cooked and my arms turn into yellow mush. It is an alarming change, but I try not to let it bother me, thinking there must be a mistake, that I am seeing things. When my husband comes home, he is upset.

"What the hell happened?" he asks.

"I'm a little under the weather," I explain. "I haven't been sleeping well. I'm still getting used to motherhood, I guess."

He rubs his ear the same way he did when we briefly broke up in our first year of dating.

"Right," he says, looking unconvinced. "It's motherhood, is it?"

"It's fine," I say, patting his head reassuringly.

He scoops up the baby and insists I take the night off. He thinks if I get some rest I will be back to my old self by morning. I protest that I can handle the baby, that I don't need his help, but he has my son in his arms and won't let go. I realize maybe a rest will be good for me. I haven't had one since my son was born four or so months ago. I held him to my chest while shaking with the flu. I rocked him to sleep when I could only limp because my joints had become swollen and stiff. I am no longer acquainted with rest.

I've always enjoyed a long bubble bath, but it doesn't seem wise to take one in my current condition, so instead I curl up in the fridge between the milk and the cold cuts, thinking of this as a low-rent spa-day type of thing, only without the cucumbers on my eyes. I stay there all night, hoping I will wake up feeling fresh and restored, but this doesn't happen. I am still a scrambled egg, warm to the touch. My husband looks disappointed when he shuffles out to the kitchen and opens the fridge.

"I think it might be time to get medical attention," he says, peering in.

"I don't think it's necessary," I reply. "I don't have time for never-ending MRIs or blood tests. I have a baby to take care of."

"But how?" he asks. "You don't seem to be at full strength."

He is speaking carefully, choosing words meant not to upset me. It's true that I am not physically capable of much in this state. But I have faced adversity in my life and this will be no different.

I assure my husband that I will do my best, that our life will not change, that I can still be a perfectly good mother, but I don't believe the words I'm saying. Mothering has become difficult—impossible, even. In my pre-baby life, I was a cliff-scrambling adventurer who risked my life daily for a thrill. I had planned on hoisting this baby on my back while bouldering, but recently it has been taking all my strength to move him from the changing table to the ground.

As the days pass, my husband grows worried that life as we know it is slipping away. He flings the fridge door wide open.

"You can't live in there forever," he shouts.

But I am not the only one who has changed. Since this baby was born, my husband's eyebrow hairs have started to curl.

"Sure I can," I say, sliding behind a carton of cream.

"I'm staging an intervention," he replies. "I miss my wife. I can't be married to scrambled eggs anymore. You have to see a therapist."

The idea of telling a stranger my feelings makes me sick.

"What can a stranger tell me that I don't already know about myself?" I ask.

"Plenty," he says.

I tell him I don't want to go, but he mentions something about divorce, and I decide that therapy can't hurt. A few days later, he drops me off for my appointment. I compose myself just outside the door.

"You're eggs!" the therapist exclaims, as I come in.

She is one of those performative types. She wears her hair

in a loose, floppy bun with a chopstick stuck through the center. She doesn't want to give off the impression of someone who tries too hard. I feel that I know everything there is to know about her, that I should be the one paid to psychoanalyze her.

I concentrate hard in order to sit. It is difficult to maneuver without any muscles. I squeeze what I think are my glutes and carefully lower myself into the chair.

"Don't worry," she says cheerily. "Your condition is perfectly reversible."

"You've seen this before?" I ask.

"Nothing a little cognitive behavioral therapy can't fix!" she replies, sidestepping the question.

At least one part of me is glad that she is confident in her abilities, even if I would never admit that I need help. She tells me my husband has filled her in on my history.

"Early motherhood is often a time of great stress," she says. "It can bring up feelings from childhood that cause terrible physiological symptoms. Is there anything you can recall that might be affecting you? Did your parents allow space for emotions? Were they present? Did they attend to your needs?"

"I don't have issues from childhood," I lie. I didn't come here to talk about my parents. My mother is dead. I am barely in touch with my father.

Who does this stranger think she is, asking me such personal questions?

The therapist chews on the corner of her turquoise reading glasses. She seems to be trying to decide if I am a reliable narrator of my own life.

"You're holding back," she says.

"I don't understand how talking about emotional problems will cure me," I say.

"The mind is capable of strange things under stress," she replies. "Unusual symptoms like yours may manifest, but often we find the cause is a repressed traumatic experience. . . . Are you sure there's nothing you want to talk about?"

"I am sure I'm not crazy," I say, offended.

"It's best not to think in those terms," she says.

This kind of back-and-forth eats up the entire session, so the therapist gives me homework. She wants me to write about sad experiences in the hope that I will uncover something I might have repressed. I take the notebook home and make a show of journaling in front of my husband so he will think I am taking the therapy seriously:

1. When I was ten, I threw a rock up into the air and then walked toward the house. I made it just a few steps before the rock crashed down on my head. Woozy, I wobbled over to my bed and fell asleep in a warm pool of my own blood. My father discovered me and rushed me to the hospital. He told me I was as dumb as the rock that fell on my head. I saw double, so I tried to be smart about it, hanging around things that would bring me pleasure in twos. There were two ice creams, two dolls, two of my summer-camp crush, Patrick, who had whiskers like a cat. But there were also two of my dad, and I was double-scolded until my brain remembered how to see just one angry dad again.

2. When I was twenty-four, I dated a nervous pianist who made sure he always had a weapon in reach. He hid a police baton in the glove box, a brass knuckle in the toilet tank, a frozen lamb shank under a couch cushion. He said the world was a scary place and he needed to feel safe. One night I startled him awake as I let myself in. Thinking I was an intruder, he threw a deer antler at my head and gave me a concussion. I racked up three thousand dollars in hospital bills, which the pianist paid, but as soon as I got home, he complained that he could not date someone who was capable of scaring him. I told him this sounded like victim-blaming, but he broke up with me anyway.

3. When I was twenty-five, I was set up with an indie rock star by a mutual friend who was his producer. The indie rock star liked women who would put warm socks on his feet before bed. The socks needed to be toasted in the oven—never the microwave. We met at a diner for our first date, and I was surprised to find another woman waiting for him. It was unclear if we were both auditioning for the sock job or if he expected each of us to put a sock on one foot at the same time. I could see Becky trying to work out the same questions as we sipped our Veselka milkshakes and bumbled through an awkward conversation. The rock star arrived half an hour late and didn't spend much time getting to know us before he asked if we

wanted to work together. He said he liked us equally, that we both seemed good at socks. Becky was willing to do a three-way job, but I was not.

4. When I was twenty-nine, I met a man who kissed with his eyelids instead of his lips. He made nature documentaries about emperor penguins and was rarely at home living among humans. I wasn't sure if I felt attracted to him, but I wanted to meet the penguins, so I kept seeing him. Then, on our third date, he pulled out a machete. He said he had gotten obsessed with the ninja phone game and was now slicing fruit in real life. He thought the ninja game sounded like a fun date activity. I could see how it might have seemed fun, but the problem was that he pulled the machete out in a secluded parking structure where no one could see us and then brought the weapon uncomfortably close to my neck as he excitedly imagined us slicing bananas, papayas, coconuts, and grapes.

When the therapist reads my homework, she asks me if seeing the machete sent me into fight-or-flight mode, if the deer antler damaged my trust in others, if the rock affected the part of my brain responsible for processing emotion. I shrug, surprised she is taking my lies seriously. At the end of the session she says that I might not be in touch with my feelings, that this might be precisely why I have turned into scrambled eggs.

* * *

MY HUSBAND ASKS HOW the second appointment went. He is eager for any kind of breakthrough.

"We're getting into a rhythm," I say.

"Maybe after a few more sessions, you will get some of your flesh back," he says. "Maybe we can, well, you know . . ."

He trails off and winks at me. I don't blame him for wanting to have sex again. It has been months. We spend the night bingeing *Yellowjackets,* and then I retreat into the fridge between the leftover bread pudding and the carton of raspberry yogurt drink.

"Miss you so much," he calls out.

He eyes me mournfully as he shuts the fridge door. I hear the baby's loud cries in the other room. They cause me physical pain, make me feel nauseous. I am a useless parent. I cannot help this child right now. It's a good thing my husband is able to console him, though the baby cries for several agonizing minutes first. The screams make my flesh feel like it's being torn from my body. I talk myself through some deep-breathing exercises and then give myself messages of affirmation, a suggestion from my therapist.

You are okay. Nothing is wrong. You will be yourself again. One day the baby's cries won't hurt anymore.

In the morning, I decide I am tired of sleeping in the fridge. I am sick of not being able to hold my child. I am sick of being scrambled eggs. I would like for my life to go back to normal. I am already at peace with the fact that some things will never be the same: I will not look refreshed in the morning; I will no longer look ten years younger than my age. I will not be able to fly to Berlin whenever I feel like it. I will not be able to have five consecutive thoughts before the baby screams. But I could get my body back. I could have functioning arms and legs. I could scramble up cliffs again. I could recognize myself in the mirror.

I retrieve the notepad and challenge myself to be honest about the trauma that I have experienced. It takes me a long time to begin writing. I lost my mother when I was thirteen to an aggressive form of cancer. By the time she was diagnosed, the illness had taken over most of her body. They couldn't tell where it had started. Cancer of the Everything. They gave her weeks to live, but the strange thing was that my mother looked just fine. Strong, even.

"Would a sick person do yoga?" she asked, wiping the sweat off her brow.

"Would a sick person walk ten miles uphill?" she asked, stretching out her hamstrings.

"Would a sick person run sprints?" she asked, lacing up her new high-performance shoes.

One night, she died after her sprints—around midnight, while I was asleep. My father removed my mother from our house so I wouldn't see her. He had a strange way of dealing with sadness. He never mentioned her again. He communicated through his eyes that I was never to bring her up either. We moved from Portland to Marin County and started a new two-person life. We bought new furniture my mother had never used, went to stores she had never visited, and generally acted as if she had never existed. By the time I was done with high school, I had almost convinced myself that I had dreamed up my mother, that it had always been just my father and me.

I tear up as I think about my mother putting on her running shoes with stage-four cancer. I have a few photos of her, stored in a box beneath my bed. I pull them out for the first time since I was thirteen and am surprised to see I am now older than her. She has no wrinkles; she glows; her hair is full and her legs are taut. It hits me differently now that I am old enough to realize how young she was when she died. She became a mother at nineteen, then fell ill at thirty-two. When did she get to live? Did she get to scale cliffs or make art? Did she enjoy being a mother? Did she get pregnant on purpose? I will never know the answers to these questions. She will forever be the person who smiled at me moments before she laced up her running shoes and died.

Now that I have a baby, I realize I have an irrational fear of orphaning my son. I never worried about dying before I had him, but suddenly I am so worried that I may have given myself a condition. What if I am scrambled eggs for the rest of my life? Will I pretend to be strong for his sake?

I bring these concerns into the next session. The therapist breathes a sigh of relief that we no longer have to bullshit and that I am serious about confronting my trauma.

"Now that we know what you've been repressing, we can start to work through your unresolved grief," she says.

"How?" I ask.

She thinks for a moment and I worry I've stumped her, that my problems are too big for therapy to fix. But then she suggests I stage a funeral for my mother and my younger self, since I never got to mourn either of these losses. I bring this idea up to my husband, expecting he will laugh, but he thinks we should try it. We wear our blackest blacks—band shirts we have lovingly never washed—and head with our son down to the cemetery. My husband picks out a pair of graves we can use for our ceremony. He thanks Thelma and Felicity for lending us their headstones. Thelma is standing in for my mother and Felicity for young me. I had prepared a sentimental speech, but I tear it into shreds and sprinkle the pieces of my speech like flower petals over the graves.

"My dad taught me to swallow my feelings," I tell my husband. "I'm eggs because I haven't dealt with them."

"Feelings never go away," he says.

I vow to take the exercise seriously so I will be cured.

The baby begins to fuss. He gets bored easily and requires a pace of life I am still getting accustomed to, a life that does not allow me to linger. My husband takes the baby for a walk around the cemetery loop and gives me a few minutes alone to grieve. I don't have much time. I won't have much time for years. I have to make it good. As soon as he turns away, I feel the tears that should have come out long ago. I have spent my life trying to stay strong. I have not allowed myself to grieve. All of it comes out now: the sadness of being a motherless daughter, of being a motherless mom. It feels good to let it out.

The next morning, I expect to wake up myself again, but I still don't recognize my image in the mirror. I feel lied to by the therapist, but maybe it takes time and I need to trust the process. A few years pass. My baby turns five, then seven, then nine. I am still waiting to wake up as myself.

EVERYTHING DISAPPEARS WHEN YOU'RE HAVING FUN

I get a text message from a number I don't recognize. **Come get the chair**, it says. **Who is this?** I ask. **Do you sell many chairs on Craigslist?** he writes.

I know who he is now. An early-thirties guy who goes by the name Turtle, with a squeaky voice, faded-pink curly hair, and a nose piercing. I sold him an office chair for twenty bucks late last year. It was a cheap blue mid-century modern chair that gave me terrible back pain. I bought it online because it looked cute. I had no idea it was poorly designed. Maybe I shouldn't have sold a stranger a backbreaking chair, but it was either that or send it to a landfill.

He sends me another message.

You NEED to take this chair back, he writes. **NOW.**

I'm a television producer, very busy. There are shows that need my notes, not enough hours in the day. I am lucky when I have time to drink a glass of water; I am lucky if I notice I am thirsty. Hollywood jobs have always required a sacrifice. Back when I started out as a production assistant, I worked sixteen-hour days. They called it paying one's dues. Working hard has served me well. I am now an executive producer—so busy I don't have time to date or have much of a social life. My only friends are the people who work for me. It's a little bit lonely, but I like the success. I'd rather be an executive producer than a wife.

Turtle must not work in the industry. He doesn't seem to understand what it's like to be busy, because he bombards me with messages about the chair.

I'm not messing around, he writes. **You'll be sorry if you don't come get it.**

I'm deep in conversation with an editor when these texts come through. We are editing a show about bees who play soccer and the beekeepers who look after them. Scientists have recently discovered that bees know how to play sports. It is difficult to capture the games on camera, so most of our footage involves the beekeepers explaining how they play. They tell us the bees are kicking soccer balls that are so small we can't see them on TV. The bites are convincing, but I need more shots of the bees buzzing by the goals to sell this game.

"I should be able to see the ball," I tell the editor.

"But the ball doesn't exist," he says.

"Pull me a few shots to choose from," I tell him, spinning around in my chair. "I'm sure there are better ones."

"It's amazing they have time to play soccer when they're going extinct," he says.

I don't know what he's getting at, so I ignore his comment.

The editor sets to work piecing together a more believable game of bee soccer as I bark out a series of orders. Unfortunately, Turtle won't stop texting me. I silence my phone. I need to focus on the storytelling. I need this to be the greatest game of bee soccer anyone's ever seen.

I leave work at eleven-thirty P.M., pepper spray in hand. My office is in the heart of Hollywood. It is not as glamorous as it sounds. Every few weeks, someone gets stabbed. There's a mental-illness epidemic that is worsening. People have urges they can't suppress. We have a security guard in front of the building, but he is able to stop only 80 percent of incidents. I walk quickly to my car, finger on the switch.

When I pull up outside my home, I see Turtle sitting on my stoop, next to the chair. He doesn't look threatening, but it's disconcerting that he would show up at my place a year after buying the chair. I park down the street, hop a fence, and sneak in through my back door. I sleep with the pepper spray under the covers, ready in case he enters. Turtle is there on the stoop in the morning but this time in different clothes—a rainbow-striped sweater I would wear. Now that it is daylight, I have the courage to confront him. I come out with a baseball bat and ask him what he wants.

"I still haven't recovered," Turtle complains.

"Must have been some backache," I say.

"It wasn't a backache," he replies, glaring at me. "What kind of person would sell a chair like that anyway?" He says this to me as if I made it. He doesn't seem to understand that once I had purchased this junk, there was no good place to put it.

Before I can ask him more questions, he runs down the street and abandons the chair. I'm late for work, but I drag it up to the second story, where I live, and kick the chair down the hallway inside my apartment. I leave it in a corner in my home office, which I'm rarely in since I'm always at work.

A few weeks later, my associate producer, Vic, comes over and sits in the chair. As soon as he sits down, he vanishes. I shout for him, but he is gone, nothing left of him. Vic turns up two days later, swimming in the Pacific hundreds of miles from the coast of Indonesia, clinging to an old refrigerator that has been washed out to sea. A cruise liner spots him and alerts the Coast Guard. The rescue is dramatic, streamed live on YouTube. Everyone in my office watches, transfixed. We clap as they fish him out of the ocean. He is given a warm blanket and is interviewed on the way to the hospital. He tells a reporter he followed a trail of plastic bottles out to the cruise liner. He returns to work a few weeks later, after he gets out of the hospital. He is banged up, shivering. He still smells like kelp. He has no idea how he ended up in the ocean. I don't tell him it was the chair.

I realize I have a problem on my hands. The chair is a liability. I can't keep it in my apartment. What if I accidentally sit on it and end up in the middle of the Pacific Ocean?

The Craigslist guy's address isn't hard to find. He has a unique name, Turtle Dobbins. I track him down on those websites that publish private information scraped off the dark web. It turns out that he lives just eleven blocks away. I wheel the chair down the street, intending to leave it on his porch, but he's sitting out front. His house looks kind of haunted. It could use some touch-up paint.

"This is your chair," I tell him. "You made it weird. You take responsibility for it."

"I didn't make it weird," he tells me. "The first time I sat down in this chair, it sent me to an iceberg melting off the coast of Greenland. I had to chew on my arm to stay awake. I lost the ends of my toes from frostbite." He scowls at me. "It's your fault."

I take a moment to absorb his accusation.

"I'm sorry to hear about your toes," I tell him. "But the chair developed these powers in your custody. It's not my fault that you lost the ends of your toes. The chair only gave me backaches."

I roll the chair toward him, but he stands up and backs away.

"Don't you dare bring that near me," he says, his voice squeaking.

He attempts to push me and the chair away from him as one unit. I cross my arms and make myself firm, the way my cat does when he doesn't want to get off my lap. I will not be moved. I will not go home with the chair. But we both know this game is dangerous.

"There's only one solution," I tell him finally. "We split custody. I'll take it Monday to Thursday. You take it Friday to Sunday. We'll share the responsibility."

"You're crazy," he says.

"Maybe so," I tell him. I roll it toward him and dash off. "See you next week," I call over my shoulder.

I FIND THE CHAIR back in front of my apartment on Monday morning. Turtle has kept it all weekend, following the terms of our agreement. Since he did his part, it's only fair that I do mine. At the end of the week, I wheel the chair eleven blocks over to his house. He's on his stoop waiting for me, eating a bowl of Lucky Charms cereal. He wears a yellow turtleneck and black suspenders with his slacks. Nearby, a leaf blower sends a neighbor's leaves into his yard. The noise makes it difficult to have a conversation. The machine kicks up some dust and I sneeze.

As I push the chair closer to him, he shrinks away. I give it a hard shove and run back to my house. He pulls the same move when he drops it off on Sunday. It takes us a few weeks of this behavior before we trust each other enough to linger at the drop-off and chitchat. I tell Turtle about my work, and he listens while I talk. He asks me if I'm happy working so much. I've never been asked this question and I have no idea how to answer it.

"Why wouldn't I be happy?" I ask. I can't imagine what I'd be doing if I weren't working every minute of my life. I'd be poor, I guess.

"There's more to life . . ." he says, trailing off.

"Is there?" I ask.

He doesn't answer.

One Friday morning, he says he's been thinking about our arrangement.

"It's no good," he says. "I don't feel safe with the chair in my house."

"I know what you mean," I say. "It's only a matter of time before I accidentally sit in it."

"We should get rid of it," he says.

We kick around the idea of returning it to the manufacturer.

"Do you have an assistant?" Turtle asks.

I tell him I have a virtual assistant named Dub. I've never met him. He lives in Vegas. His avatar is a picture of a cartoon dog. He's been working with me for only three months. My old assistant, Lil Bev, could have handled the chair. She sat outside my office in real life. She got everything done, but when she quit for a job that offered health insurance, the production company told me that we couldn't afford full-fleshed assistants anymore. I thought I would be fine with a virtual one, but Dub's work is spotty at best. I'm always wondering if he's at a bar when he's not answering emails. I've thought about letting him go, but he is technically not my employee, not under my control. He works for an employment agency. It feels weird not being able to verify that he is working all sixteen hours of his day, paying his dues like I did. But then I remember he's not paying dues, because he's unlikely to be promoted.

"Maybe he can dispose of it, then?" Turtle asks.

Even though I am skeptical Dub will be able to deal with the chair, I know Turtle is right. I can't spend the rest of my life shuttling it down the street. Someone could sit in it. And what if Turtle moves? What if I move? We need to find a permanent solution.

Dub, I need help, I text. I send him Turtle's address and ask him to send the chair back to its manufacturer. And make sure no one sits in it, I text.

Sure thing, he writes. Might take a day or two.

That's fine, I tell him. Turtle puts it out on his front porch with caution tape and a note that says DO NOT SIT.

* * *

ON SUNDAY, TURTLE TEXTS me that the chair is gone.

You're a godsend, I text Dub. **Thanks for dealing with the chair.**

You are very welcome, he texts back. **I like to be of assistance.**

It's taken care of? I ask.

Yes, Ms. Roo. The chair won't be bothering you anymore. I promise.

He reminds me I have a meeting starting in a few minutes. I connect to the Zoom link he sends, but no one else joins. It turns out I don't have a meeting. It's Sunday. I work so much that all the days seem the same.

I'm very sorry, Dub texts. **I have made a mistake. This meeting is scheduled for tomorrow morning.**

I need you on the ball, I text him. **I can't be showing up to meetings that don't exist.**

He doesn't reply to this message, but a few hours later he sends me a text. **Shitfuck** is all it says, even though he never swears.

Is this intended for me? I ask.

He doesn't respond.

Shitfuck? I ask. **Really, Dub?**

Still no response.

TURTLE IS SITTING ON my porch when I go outside to water my mint. I ask him why he is here now that the chair is gone. He looks down at his dirty sneakers and lingers. I wonder if he is here because his house is haunted. Maybe if he fixed it up a little bit, he would want to spend more time there. He tells me he misses our old routine. Now he has no reason to see me.

"Maybe we could share custody of something else?" Turtle asks.

I wonder if he's flirting. He seems like the kind of guy who could really use a girlfriend. If he had a girlfriend, he would know not to let his house get haunted. I invite him in so we can think up some ideas for something to share. He shivers as he walks up the stairs. It's not that cold in here. I look through my messy living room for an object of interest. I hold up a Tortoise record, an old bent spoon I found on a sidewalk in Hungary, a doodled-in early edition of *Jane Eyre,* a hand-carved wood doll that my father got on a trip to South Africa.

"Did you offer the Tortoise record because I'm Turtle?" he asks shyly.

"It's a good record," I say. "I thought you would like it."

He has a nice, compact smile. Just moves the corners of his lips. He pockets the doll and says it is perfect. He says he will bring the doll back tomorrow. *Or you could stay,* I almost say. I realize I enjoy his company.

"You're different than I imagined," I tell him. "For a guy who texts in all caps."

"I only do that when I'm really mad," he says.

"I thought you were deranged," I say. "You should work on first impressions. Like your house."

"I haven't gotten around to fixing it up," he says. "I've been busy."

He has an expression on his face that I cannot parse. I make us drinks in copper mugs. I bought them at the flea market ten years ago, thinking they would be cute on a date, but have never had an occasion to use them because I am so busy with my job. Now I am single at a weird age and I have only myself to blame for letting the mugs collect dust.

Turtle takes off his shoes and sits down on my floor, his back pressed against my wall. I join him. There are strange sounds emanating from the apartment below—of running and giggling. I imagine my downstairs neighbor has friends over for a naked pillow fight, though I'm not sure what he is doing. Most people's fun sounds different than his. He had a mental breakdown once, or so I thought based on the number of things I heard shattering. I hear everything private in his life, but when we cross paths outside, we nod and say hi and pretend like we are strangers.

Turtle thinks my neighbor is playing Exquisite Corpse. I've never heard of this parlor game. He describes it as somewhere between Telephone and Pictionary. I tell him I want to play the game with him sometime, though I want to play a version that involves corpses. He smiles. Then he becomes quiet. He is looking down the hallway, toward my bedroom for some reason. Maybe the sounds are triggering.

"I think maybe I have PTSD," he says.

"From waking up on an iceberg or something else?" I ask.

"Iceberg," he says. I scoot closer to him. "They told me I was adrift for seventy-six hours. It was a long time to think I would die. I didn't expect anyone to find me there. I thought I would either freeze or sink into the ocean. It's a good thing there was an oil tanker around."

I rub my forehead as I picture him alone. Poor Turtle, clinging to the melting iceberg. So many ways he could have died. If only I hadn't sold him the chair. He pulls off his socks and shows me his sad little frostbite toes.

"I don't know why I feel responsible," I tell him. "The chair wasn't like that when I sold it to you. I sat in it every day. I'm sorry you had that experience, though. It sounds difficult."

He doesn't absolve me of guilt as I'd hoped. Instead, he stares at a print of a hot-air balloon that hangs on a wall across the room.

"PTSD is not what I thought it was," he tells me. "My nervous system thinks I'm in danger when I think I'm relaxed on the couch. It's stuck in fight-or-flight. I'm always startled, my cheek twitches, my fingers forget how to work, I can't grasp a butter knife. I'm still working through it."

"Let me know what I can do to help," I say.

"It's better now that the chair is out of my life," he says. "I can move on."

"I want to help your nerves calm down," I say. "Maybe you need a massage."

"Maybe," he says.

I put my arm around him to offer comfort and start to rub his shoulders. But then my neighbor screams, "Beans!!!" at the top of his lungs and ruins everything. Turtle is startled again. I lead him into my bedroom, where it is quieter. He stays the night and sleeps in my arms, but nothing happens, and I realize soon after he leaves that I'm disappointed.

I GO A FEW days without hearing from Dub. He doesn't book any meetings. I have to book them myself. Finally, I text to ask if he's feeling ill. I ask if he sat in the chair. Did he ignore my warning? Did he drive out to Los Angeles to move the chair himself? I search the news for reports of a man lost at sea, a man shipwrecked on an iceberg, a man trapped in an oil spill, a man clinging to a satellite that is falling back to earth. There is no report of anyone turning up in some environmental disaster, no news cameras standing by for a live break-in that will boost ratings.

I start to feel guilty as it becomes clear something bad has happened to my assistant. Turtle is upset. He thinks we have killed him.

"I am sure Dub is in a better place," I say. "Let's imagine he quit for a job that gave him health insurance and a pension. Maybe an in-person job, where he can have friends who care about him. He wouldn't have driven here. There's no way he sat in it."

"Sure," Turtle says, but he is not convinced.

As the days wear on, I worry that Dub is dead.

Turtle decides he won't feel okay unless we find him. He thinks we should take a road trip to Vegas and look for him. Normally I don't have time to leave town for the weekend, but it is my fault that my assistant is missing, so I agree to go with him. I'm eager to get to know Turtle better. I figure this trip will be good for him. Maybe it will cure him of his PTSD. Maybe if I can help him relax, I won't be just a destroyer of lives but a fixer too. It's like carbon offsetting but with ethics.

I pick him up on Saturday morning. He grabs his Ativan and a pair of swim trunks. On the way, we stop at the gas station for some Cokes and licorice. Turtle leans back in the passenger seat with his sneakers on the dashboard. He searches Travelocity.com and books a room at a hotel with a giant pool. This is the kind of task Dub would have taken care of for me—though he would have booked me a smoking room despite my allergy to smoke particles.

As we cross the state line, Turtle unfolds a map he bought at the gas station. We don't need a map, but he says he likes props.

"Props?" I ask.

"Real things you can hold in your hands," he says. "They make me feel grounded."

"Have you been to Vegas?" I ask.

Turtle shakes his head. "I'm not a fan of sun or sin."

I ask why he lives in Los Angeles if he doesn't like sun or sin. He tells me he was born in that haunted house. His mother birthed him in the tub. I ask if he still lives with his mother. He nods but then tells me she's dead.

"Maybe that's why you have PTSD," I say.

"No, it's the chair," he insists. He is quiet for a minute. "You have Dub's address? I'll plug it into Google Maps."

"I don't have it," I say.

Turtle frowns.

"So how are we supposed to find him?"

"Good question," I say.

Dub's been my assistant for three months, but I have no idea what he looks like. I've only seen his cartoon-dog avatar. Turtle wonders how it is possible I have never seen a photo of him. I remind him that Dub is a virtual assistant. I haven't even talked to him on the phone.

I can describe what my old assistant looks like. I knew Lil Bev in real life. I saw her cry when her boyfriend cheated on her. She brought me cupcakes on my birthday. Dub has only booked me meetings.

Turtle finds Dub's Instagram, which is spare, as expected. A few pictures of the desert. One of a McDonald's and another of a laundromat. He searches the handle and finds things that may be adjacent to Dub. A picture of Jerry Stahl, a movie poster for *Harold and Maude*. A picture of some dirty children's cowboy boots. A paintbrush.

"He's an artist," Turtle says.

He's decided Dub paints monsters and sells his artwork to a boutique children's clothing store.

"How old do you think he is?" Turtle asks.

"Not a millennial," I say. "He uses two spaces after periods."

"He might be a boomer, then," Turtle says.

"Maybe," I say. "But he's good with apps. Just bad at remembering stuff. I think he responds to half of my requests."

"Maybe he's in high school," Turtle says. Then later he says quietly, "I guess I don't reply to emails either. He could be a millennial."

"We've really narrowed it down," I say.

We arrive at the hotel in the early afternoon. I try not to look at the dirty old carpet inside the casino when we check in. The carpet feels like the saddest part of my soul, like gum smashed into pavement. I think of an uncle who had lost his life savings in a Vegas casino when I was a kid. My parents had written him a large check to help him get back on his feet, but he spent it at the slot machines. I have disliked Vegas since then.

On our way to the elevator, I think I see a zombie, but when I get closer I realize I'm looking at an elderly lady walking backward unsteadily; I've mistaken her loose bun for a face.

A man in neon board shorts hovers near us with a drink in each hand. He is chewing on a cocktail umbrella, which he must have removed from one of his drinks. There is a sunburn in the shape of a cloud on his chest.

"Dub?" Turtle asks.

The man shakes his head and takes a sip of one of his cocktails before moving on. I tell Turtle that Dub wouldn't be hanging out in a casino. He is not a tourist here, like us.

AFTER WE DROP OFF our bags and freshen up, we jump back into the car. We start by driving around on the strip, then branch out into the surrounding neighborhoods. Turtle has developed a theory that Dub lives between a McDonald's and a laundromat. We drive to every McDonald's in Vegas and ask if anyone knows Dub. I show them photos of the avatar. The cashiers shake their heads. But Turtle is only getting more excited.

"There has to be a clue you're forgetting," he says. "Something that will lead us to him."

I think for a bit. Most of our exchanges were about meetings and phone calls. Calendar entries. I text Sadman, a fellow executive producer who shares Dub. He writes that he barely talked to him but says he will ask his associate producer, Cowly. He thinks they were friends.

We follow a short, mutton-chopped pedestrian in brown bell-bottoms for two blocks. He looks over his shoulder nervously as we trail him. He starts to wave his arms, then pulls out a knife as he hurries down the street. We find someone else to follow. His face looks sort of doggish. He has pointy ears. Turtle calls out for Dub, but the man doesn't turn to look at us.

Sadman then gets back to me with new information. He says that Cowly thinks Dub owns a saloon just outside the city. She has the name and address. A real lead, finally.

WE PULL UP TO the saloon. It makes sense that a guy with a cartoon-dog avatar would own this bar, I tell Turtle, as I lead us in through the double doors. He nods. We get a couple of whiskey sours and ask the bartender if we can talk to the owner.

A woman comes out from the back. She is mid-thirties, wearing vegan-leather pants and star pasties.

"Dub?" I ask, surprised.

"Shauna," she says.

"Do you work as a virtual assistant?" Turtle asks.

"What's a virtual assistant?" she replies.

I text Sadman that he has given us bad intel. He writes that he has just looked up Dub's temp company and learned that Dub is an AI bot. Dub disappeared after the server experienced an outage. He says the information was buried in the fine print, at the bottom of the page, long past the point where everyone would stop reading. The company prefers to present their employees as real people.

"That explains a lot," Turtle says, nodding.

Unlike Turtle, I struggle to absorb the news. Dub had seemed human to me.

I text Sadman for proof that Dub is a bot. He sends us the

site he found. Apparently, the virtual assistants come with fake backstories, hence the saloon. Turtle wonders what happened to the chair. I scroll down and see that the bots subcontract work out to humans for manual labor. It's possible that someone else sat in that chair, but I decide not to mention this possibility to Turtle. What could we do to help that person? I tell myself that it's unlikely the subcontractor would have sat on it. The next person to sit in the chair would be someone I couldn't imagine—so many degrees of separation between us that this person might as well not exist.

"Feel better?" I ask Turtle.

"Yeah," he says.

"Now we can finally have fun," I say.

I slip my hand in his. He winks at me, then smiles. I have given him this levity. I have unburdened him. It is the best gift I can give him.

I order us another pair of whiskey sours and feel better as the night goes on. Shauna hands us the drinks. It tickles me to think of Turtle with a cocktail or two in him. I want to know what he's like when he's not so shy. He is starting to glow, thanks to the neon cow lit up behind him.

I suck the last bits of juice out of an old lemon wedge, toss the rind into my drink, and kiss him. He looks surprised at first, but then he kisses me back. His lips taste good. I chew on them for a bit. We abandon the car in the saloon parking lot and walk several miles to the hotel, hand in hand, smooching the whole way.

It's three A.M. by the time we get to our hotel. Instead of going inside, we head to the pool and cast off our clothes. Our pants look silly without us. There are other couples frolicking at the edges, but this pool is so large it is easy to forget they are there. We make out under the Vegas lights. The neon shows off an opulence built upon people's ruin.

I tell Turtle I wish we were out in nature and not in a manmade pool behind a fake Roman palace. We float down the lazy river on our backs and pretend we are on a real river. Then Turtle tells me there are pink river dolphins in the Amazon. He saw them on a nature documentary about Peru. I've seen this "nature documentary" too—it's one of Sadman's shows. Because I am not always truthful about the soccer skills of bees, I assume the pink dolphins aren't real. But Turtle insists that they exist. He runs naked back to his phone at the edge of the pool, pulls up an article, and tells me four facts about them while shivering.

"Fact one: The pink river dolphin can change colors. They're born gray and turn pink as they age. Fact two: Pink river dolphins are shy—they spend a lot of time underwater and rarely make themselves known. Fact three: Pink river dolphins can swim upside down. Fact four: They impregnate women at night."

He looks up at me, no longer so sure if they are real.

I tell Turtle we should go see for ourselves. I want the pink dolphins to be real as much as he does. I have gotten invested in them.

Then I realize that I can't go to Peru. Work is piling up. There are no redundancies built into the schedule. I've probably already been gone long enough to be fired. I imagine my editor lost and wandering the halls, looking for direction. He will bump into the company president, who will take over the cut and realize I am expendable. It is possible that by the time I arrive back in Los Angeles, my job will have been eliminated. A lifetime of hard work will be flushed down the toilet.

This wasn't how I pictured my future when I moved to Hollywood. I thought there would be a time I could relax and enjoy my life after getting promoted, but I've needed to hustle to keep my job. I don't have sick days or health insurance. I'm one catastrophe away from losing everything. It makes me nervous to live like this as I get older, but I can't see an alternative.

Turtle sets his head on my shoulder, content. He looks happier than he did the day I first met him, before he sat in that chair. When we get back to the room, we book tickets to Peru.

TRASH HEAP HERO

Nit works at the trash heap, putting out fires. She didn't go to firefighter school, but ever since the landfill was relocated to her town twelve years ago, so many fires break out that they need extra hands. She makes up for her lack of training with enthusiasm. She wanted to become a regular firefighter, but the fire department wouldn't hire a woman. Putting out trash heap fires is her only shot. She prizes her uniform, a jumpsuit she sewed herself. She chose an olive fabric to contrast with the orange flames. She hangs it on her wall so it is the first thing she sees when she wakes up and the last thing she sees before she falls asleep.

Nit is the only firefighter who is fit enough to climb to the top of the heap. The easiest route is up the side on an electric scooter, but the quicker route involves climbing the fast-food slime. The rest of the firefighters use this route to slide down. Sometimes, as Nit works, she finds children climbing on the heap. They like the landfill because it is full of shiny robot toys, often with batteries still in. There are so many American toys in the landfill that it looks like a playground. Who could blame the children for sneaking in? The trash heap is the most interesting attraction in the town. She leads the children back to their homes and promises to collect the best toys for them. The kids call her Auntie Firefighter. This is the closest she will come to having children.

Nit's mind is always on her work. Being on all the time allows her to be good at her job. She's won an award this year: Most Fires Put Out at the Top of the Trash Heap. She likes having a job that is making a difference.

As she walks around town, she likes to imagine whose trash she has seen. The medal of honor could belong to the stoic old man who stands outside the bakery. The dresser with the blue plastic knobs could belong to the teenage girl who delivers noodles. She knows the trash comes from far away, but it is better to imagine it discarded by her fellow townspeople. This trash would be a burden they should share. The necessary byproducts of living.

NORMALLY THE TRASH HEAP grows little by little, but one day it triples in size and there is a new, plastic smell emanating. The summit is filled with milk jugs and water bottles. Nit asks the man with the clipboard if the new trash has come from Bangkok. Bangkok is not her community, but it is still close enough that she can accept the trash as theirs. The man shrugs. He doesn't have an answer for her. Later that day, he gets drunk on the job and tells her that the plastic money goes into his pockets. He says that he plans to use it to buy his family a nice house with flushing toilets. The government gets rich off it. She goes home with a terrible headache from the plastic fumes, but she is back a few days later when a new fire breaks out, this time at the summit. The rush she gets from climbing the heap is enough for her to battle through the fumes. She likes a challenge. The headache forces her to take a break, but she puts the fire out.

THE FOLLOWING WEEK, HER mother calls to say her pet bird is paralyzed. Nit offers to buy her mother a new bird, but her mother isn't satisfied with this response. She says the bird is not the point. The point is that the trash heap fumes are toxic.

"You need to find a new job," says her mother. "The trash heap isn't good for you."

"I like how my life is going," Nit says. "I do important work."

"How long can you put out fires anyway?" her mother asks. "You are getting old, endangering yourself. Trash is a young man's game, and now they've dumped plastic on it. It's not the same trash you like."

"It is not a man's game at all," Nit says. "If it were a man's game, one of those men would be able to reach the top."

"I wish they had never started that landfill," her mother complains. "All you ever do is brag about how many fires you've put out, how many times you've been to the top, how many men you've beaten."

It's true Nit is happier as a firefighter. Before she had this job, she felt lost. The girls at school threw rocks at her because she dressed like a boy. The boys were angry when she outran them on the soccer field. Sometimes she bit them when they said mean things. She was sent to a school for girls after she ripped the corner of a boy's ear off with her teeth. On her thirteenth birthday, no one from school wanted to come to her party, so she ran twenty kilometers through the muddy trails alone, blinking back sweaty tears. That was when she first knew that she would have an irregular life, but she vowed to have an interesting one. She thought maybe she would travel the world and climb the tallest mountains in the Americas or Nepal. This isn't quite the life she pictured, but it is a meaningful one.

She feels restless in between jobs. There are no mountains nearby that aren't made of trash. She doesn't have the money to travel, so firefighting is what she has. Every time she puts out a fire, she hopes for a new one to break out.

ON NIT'S THIRTY-FIFTH BIRTHDAY, her mother takes her to get scrubbed. They sit in tubs of boiling water while elderly ladies tend to them. Nit is shocked that her mother is willing to sit naked in this room. Normally she is modest, but she will do anything to ensure that Nit is smoothed. A short, spotted woman brings over a bucket full of cleaning stones.

"Make sure to get under the armpits," her mother says.

The elderly woman nods.

Nit winces as the older woman scrubs her with the coarse

stones. The older woman works hard to rub the toughness out of her.

"You are pretty underneath all of the soot," the woman says, surprised.

"She prefers to make herself ugly," Nit's mother says. "She used to wear shoes made of duct tape. Now she only wears shoes on the trash heap."

Nit's mother shivers. Her tub has gotten too cold. A pink-haired child, maybe ten years old, pours a bucket of hot water over Nit's mother's head to warm her. Nit recognizes the child from the trash heap. A few years ago, she'd found a bicycle and had worked hard to untangle it from yards of cassette tape ribbon. Nit remembers the child because the bike was tangled in Michael Jackson's music. Nit had used her firefighting tools to free the bike from the ribbon and helped the child walk it back to her house.

"Are you still enjoying the bike?" Nit asks.

"I ride it everywhere," the pink-haired girl says, gazing at Nit. "It is a rich person's bicycle. And now I'm rich."

Nit's mother's face is full of hope as she sees Nit's pink, raw skin emerge, but in a matter of days a new fire breaks out, and Nit's face is sooty and happy again.

THE LARGEST FIRE RAGES in the landfill's fifteenth year. It's at the top of the trash heap, which now reaches ninety-five meters high. The smoke is thicker than usual. Nit develops an intense headache as she approaches. She ascends using the slime route, pulling herself up by a rope she has left tied to the top. Her boots have good soles to grip the trash, and her core is strong. She is proud of how quick and sure-footed she is, even on the most challenging route, even as the fumes should slow her down. She will put out these fires no matter how high this trash heap gets, no matter what they put in it.

As she approaches the top, she loses her grip on the rope and lands on a broken computer. She has no idea how far she has fallen. She has no idea where the slime trail is now. If Nit is lost, who will rescue her? There is no one else who can make it up this far. She is the one who does the rescuing.

She stands up and rubs her hip, where she landed. Her back stiffens up. She worries her mother is right. She is too old to do what she loves. She has lost her edge. She will die on this trash heap. She's always imagined she will go out fighting a fire, but she isn't ready to die just yet. She starts to climb an unfamiliar route, her eyes burning. She scrambles up a trail made of phones, up into the flames. The last thing she remembers is her foot slipping out from under her.

SHE WAKES UP IN the hospital, her body wrapped in gauze. There are burns on her arms, legs, and head. She has never felt so much pain. She lets out a loud scream, then another, smaller one. She has never thought about her skin before, but now it is all she can think about. The doctors tell her she fell forty meters to the ground. Luckily, she's escaped severe injuries; even her burns are minor.

Her father brings cold water and hot soup, like he is unsure which one will help.

"Oh, Nit!" he says. "I hate to see you like this, my beautiful, old little girl! Are you in much pain?"

"I am fine," she replies. "You don't have to worry about me."

He looks like he wants to hug her but hesitates and pats her head instead. This is the first time in her life she has felt delicate, the first time she has needed a second skin. Her mother stands across the room, holding her buddha pendant.

"As soon as they let her out of the hospital, she'll be right back on that heap again," she says.

"It's what she loves," her father says, throwing his hands into the air. "What are we going to do? You can't stop someone from doing what they love."

"If I don't put out these trash heap fires, who will?" Nit asks.

"Someone else will get stronger," her mother tells her. "Let them rise to the challenge."

It's difficult to breathe in her tender skin. When she sucks in a breath, she can feel the trash heap inside her. She imagines her organs have gotten tangled in Michael Jackson cassette tape ribbon. At night, in the hospital, she dreams the surgeons are working to free her kidney from the tape. They extract the ribbon and wind it back inside the cassette. She watches as the surgeons scour the heap for a boombox. The dream ends as they hit PLAY on "Pretty Young Thing."

In the morning, her father brings congee to the hospital. He tells her he wishes she would find a way to be a hero that didn't involve poisoning herself. He asks what's so great about putting out trash fires. He reminds her the trash isn't theirs anymore. It's been a long time since the trash came from Thailand. She is tending to plastic that is shipped over in containers from other countries, as part of the circular economy.

She tells him it makes no difference where the trash comes from. If she lets the fires burn, their neighbors will suffer the consequences.

Later that morning, as he cleans up the congee, he brings up the floods that had killed his grandmother. She was swept away by the waters, too frail to hold on. Nit can barely remember the floods. She was a child when they happened. At the time, it didn't make sense to her that the rain could wash away their matriarch. She was sturdy, despite being ninety.

"Why are we talking about the floods?" she asks.

"I wish for rain to put these trash fires out, but then I think of *that* disaster," he says. Nit thinks he's been struggling since losing his grandmother, that as a family they are adrift somehow, torn apart by the forces of nature.

WHILE NIT IS IN the hospital, another fire breaks out at the top of the heap. A few other firefighters attempt to summit, but they are unable to get into position even though they've spent the last several weeks practicing. It takes her twelve weeks to recover well enough to walk. The fire burns until she is healed. She knows she is out of shape after so many weeks in bed, but the longer she waits, the bigger the fire will get. She can't risk it getting out of control. She has never failed to put out a fire.

When she finally arrives at the landfill, she finds a crew at work dismantling the heap, despite the fire crackling at the top. The man with the clipboard tells her they are relocating the heap to a town twelve hours away. She is surprised that the heap can be relocated while it's on fire, but the man with the clipboard shrugs. Government's orders, he says.

He coughs but is unable to expel whatever is inside him. Nit can't help but think her mother is behind the relocation effort. The children will be sad to lose their trash heap, she thinks. There will be no source of free toys. The pink-haired girl will outgrow her bicycle, and then what? Her family will never be able to afford a bicycle from a store.

But Nit can't afford to waste too much time arguing with the man with the clipboard. She scales the northern face of the heap. Her legs still work even though they feel as though they shouldn't, even though she spent several weeks in a hospital bed. She is fueled by adrenaline. The man with the clipboard shouts that it is dangerous to climb the heap while they are dismantling it, as if it isn't dangerous to climb a trash heap that's on fire. By the time the fire is out, they've removed the slime route, and she has to take a slower way down.

EVEN AS THE HEAP dwindles and the fires no longer erupt, she visits the site every day. Soon the heap is a tiny pile of trash, like any rubbish one would find by the side of the road. Nit stares at it despondently. She can't climb the rubbish. What is she supposed to do with no fires to put out?

I can't let this ruin me, Nit tells herself. *I can't lose my self-worth.*

Once she is sure another fire won't break out on the heap, she puts in an application at the fire department. She has more experience than anyone and has won the coveted firefighting award, but they still won't take a woman.

On her way home, she passes a burning car with six men spraying their hoses all over the place. Nit can't stand how much water they're wasting. She grabs the hose and puts out the car fire in minutes. The men are angry with her. They shout at her as she drives back home. They throw rocks at her. She feels just like she did when she was a child, like no time has passed at all—like she was never a trash heap hero and is still just a strange kid with a big dream.

MONTHS PASS WITH NO work, but Nit is still a firefighter in her nerves. The fight-or-flight urge never ends. Her body is ready to go. Her legs are ready to scramble. She jumps at any sound that could signal fire. She runs into the kitchen to put out fires that don't exist. She throws a bucket of water into a sizzling wok that has generated too much smoke. She needs to find another outlet for this adrenaline, but there are not too many exciting opportunities around. She feels herself fading. She can't go on much longer without a purpose.

She thinks about going to school, but education is not the kind of purpose she seeks. She considers moving to Bangkok, but she doesn't know much about urban life. Soon she realizes she has no choice but to follow the trash heap. She will uproot her life, move away from her parents. There is no life for her without the heap.

She tells her parents at a Sunday dinner, after she has already packed up her things. Her mother is too angry to speak and paces around the kitchen. Her father erupts at the news.

"We worked so hard to raise you, and you leave us for a trash heap?" he shouts.

"It's not my fault they moved it," Nit tells him. "Maybe they'll move it back when the residents complain."

"They'll never move it back," her father says. "They'll move it farther away. You'll keep chasing it and we'll never see you again." He looks toward her mother. "This was not how having a child was supposed to go."

She feels for her father. He has always been fond of her. He relies on her. But she has herself to look after. She can't bear this empty feeling anymore.

"I'll come home to visit," she promises, though she has no idea if she will ever have enough money for the long trip home.

IN THE MORNING, SHE hops into the train compartment. She isn't sure she has boarded the correct train, but the person in charge of the transportation told her it would come at 6:02 A.M. This train came at 6:09—close enough, she thinks. It's dark inside the car. This train is transporting rice. She has left most of her possessions behind. There wasn't room in her bag to bring her award, but she has a few photos from her childhood. If there was light in this compartment, she would pull out a photo of herself at thirteen outrunning the boys on the soccer field, back when she thought maybe she could go to the Olympics, before she knew the limits of her life.

The train comes to a stop. When the compartment door opens, a bald man beckons to her.

"You're the firefighter?" the bald man asks.

She nods and hops down from the car, slinging her bag over her shoulder.

"Thank you for coming," he says. "We need you. We have many fires to put out here and no one experienced to help."

"Glad I can be of service," she says, nodding.

He drives her an hour down the road, to a house where he has rented her a room. The place is bare. It looks even emptier once she unpacks—too few things for the space—but the blank walls give her hope. There is work to do. A life to build. She will scale the new trash mountain and follow it wherever it goes. Someone has to put the fires out.

RETURN

Alice and Hien had come over to my house for drinks—one of the rare times we had managed to get together since my son, Alfie, was born. None of us had emerged from the pandemic years unscathed. Alice was depressed. Hien didn't have a clear diagnosis, but it had been two years since she had brushed her hair or zipped up her pants. She was sitting in the living room with her fly undone, trying hard to focus on the conversation.

Of the three of us, I was in the worst shape. I had recently been diagnosed with lupus—a rare complication of Covid. Suddenly I had health issues. I was still adjusting to a new life, learning how to be a mother while seeking the drugs that would get me to remission. I never had the strength to pick up my child. Supposedly one day I wouldn't be so tired and my bones wouldn't ache. I shouldn't have been drinking. I was scared the alcohol would induce a seizure when mixed with my medication. It had happened once. I took a few small sips of the cocktail Alice had made, which she assured me was mostly blood-orange juice.

I was still waiting for the buzz to hit when a commercial for Return came on the television. It promised a night of our old lives: dancing at Club Tee Gee in a striped dress and cowboy boots, a simple joy from an earlier time. I had heard about Return but never entertained the idea of using it. The app was founded by a megalomaniac who had made some controversial statements and had recently become a hero to the far right. We wanted to cancel him, but this commercial featured three women who were having the kind of fun that had eluded us. If we all chipped in, we could afford to book a trip.

Alice ordered the Return before we could change our minds. She said we were doing it for me. She wanted to see me healthy again. I couldn't remember what it was like to not feel sick. I wanted to find a way back to my old self so I could be a better mother to Alfie. After failing several drugs, I had lost hope that I would feel better.

The app gave us an estimated arrival time of thirteen minutes. I went out to say goodbye to my husband, Harold. Earlier in the evening, he'd snuck out to the garage, where he worked on secret furniture in his spare time. He never told me what he was building, but I saw the scraps on the floor. I found it amusing he thought he could hide his furniture hobby, but I understood. We had few thrills in this phase of life. It was fun to have secrets.

When Harold heard me approach, he ran out to intercept me in front of the garage. His hair was full of sawdust.

"Is Alfie up?" he asked.

"No, it's not that," I told him. "We're going out. Back late. Don't wait up."

He nodded with concern. I knew he was worried I would collapse if I went out to drink, but he let me go without protesting.

THE CAR WAS UNASSUMING, a black Toyota indistinguishable from a normal rideshare. The driver seemed on edge when we opened the door. She was in her early sixties, with a sad face but strong biceps. As we buckled ourselves in, we asked her what to expect. She said it was her first ride of this kind, that she had no idea how the time travel worked. She was planning to follow the directions provided by the app on her phone.

We made some jokes. We were in it together. She hit the START RIDE button and mounted her phone to the dashboard. As we pulled out of the neighborhood, she asked if we preferred to take the 101 or the 5. I worried we had booked the wrong kind of ride and that was why the car had come so quickly. I began to panic, thinking of the sum we had spent. But I decided any kind of night out would be worth it. I was desperate for the kind of hanging out that happened outside the walls of my house. I hadn't been to a bar since I got sick. The smallest of joys would do.

Somewhere near the exit for downtown, our driver turned around and offered us mints from a tin. Alice declined. Hien shook her head.

"You have to take one," the driver said. "The ride will stop if you don't take the mints."

I scanned my friends' faces. We had a silent conversation. Should we take the mints? Alice and Hien nodded yes. We'd paid too much money to skip the mints.

WE WOKE UP ON a sidewalk downtown, in the Arts District. The car was gone. The sky smelled like smoke; the streetlamps were flickering; the wind sounded like it was breathing. It took us a bit to get our bearings. Nothing was recognizable. I figured we must have been sent to the future, not the past. I watched Alice's eye twitch as she came to the same realization. She took out her phone and pulled up the news. She said we had traveled ahead five years.

Hien started to tweet her displeasure, but I tugged her along down the street. "The future could be cool," I told her. "We're out of the house. You zipped up your pants. I'm in a dress." I realized then that I didn't feel fatigued or stiff. I felt like my old self. Loose-limbed. Comfortable in my body. I could have run a marathon.

We decided to look for Little Easy, a New Orleans–themed bar that sold a lavender-flavored French 75. I had celebrated my thirtieth birthday in this bar with sixty or so friends I'd accumulated in my twenties, as new friendships were made at trivia night, art openings, flag-football games on the beach. All those people were scattered across the country now, working remotely from their farms. They were shaking off depression and brain fog. They'd become acquaintances. People who liked stuff on social media. Only the three of us had been left behind—three old bodies who'd felt like the burned-out tree stumps in the Angeles. I was grateful that feeling was gone now.

We turned onto Fifth and walked a few blocks. The sidewalks were packed with spinners on Peloton bikes—hundreds of exhausted cyclists pedaling fast. All of them were dressed in street clothes. Black leather skirts. Sequined bras. Hien guessed that we'd wandered into a TikTok. We walked through the spinners to get to Little Easy but found the bar shuttered. Every bar on the block was out of business.

"At least you're healthy," Alice said.

"I haven't felt this good in a long time," I told her.

I wanted to scream and pop some balloons, shatter wineglasses, run up the side of the brick wall she was leaning against. Do parkour. What to do with all this health? Could I bottle it? Take it back home with me afterward?

Our driver walked out of a bookstore across the street. She was pointing a gun at us, a half-eaten burger in her other hand. I told her we had no cash, but she said she didn't want our money. She crossed the street and waved us toward a bin of clip-in spin shoes.

"Could you stop pointing the gun at us?" Hien asked.

"I do what the app says," the driver replied. I reached into the bin and put on a pair of ill-fitting spin shoes. Under the threat of gun violence, we climbed onto Pelotons. The driver told us we could warm up for five minutes but then we would need to cycle over sixty revolutions per minute. She didn't back away until the three of us were cycling at a reasonable clip. We relaxed only when she disappeared into the bookstore across the street again.

"A workout isn't the worst idea," Hien said tentatively.

"I could use some endorphins," I agreed.

We would make the most of a bad situation. I used to work out every day before I had Alfie. I missed the easy pleasure of exercise. Thankfully, the endorphins came fast, after a few minutes. I felt strong and free. Blood pumping, neurons firing, body and mind in sync. I relished the feeling until my legs burned. I had hit my limit. I was too out of shape to push myself. I hopped off the bike. Just as soon as the wheels stopped, the streetlamp above me started flickering. The driver hurried out of the bookstore.

"See what you did?" she asked, gesturing with her gun toward a streetlight.

"Are we powering the city?" Alice asked.

Hien let up to test the hypothesis. A light in the building across the street from us went out. It came back on as soon as she got above sixty rpm. I hoisted myself onto the bike again. After a few minutes of cycling, the streetlight flicked on. The driver seemed satisfied. She went back inside. I started to feel lightheaded. I had picked a bad day to skip lunch. But I wanted to project a strong front. I'd become an actress after developing lupus. I couldn't be vulnerable, because everyone else would worry. It didn't matter how much pain I was in or how fatigued I felt. Thanks to my acting skills, few people understood I was sick.

Hien pulled out her phone and managed to find some tweets that shed light on our predicament. She said the rivers were dry. The dams didn't work.

"So we were kidnapped by the time-travel app to fix the future," Alice said.

We were the stupid ones for trusting the megalomaniac. We knew what kind of person he was before we booked a

Return. But I'd wanted my health back so badly, I was willing to look the other way.

Hien had gone pale in this time. As soon as she let up on the pedals, the driver popped out of the bookstore with her gun. We stared at the ground as we pedaled so we wouldn't see the desperation on one another's faces. The driver retreated to the bookstore.

"I'm sure there will be a break," I said.

"Do they care if we die?" Hien wondered.

I started to lose stamina around the two-hour mark. My muscles were shaking. I wondered how much of an effect I'd had on the power grid. Maybe I had allowed someone to charge their phone for five minutes. Was there really no water in the rivers?

A few bikes down, a guy fell off and hit the ground. Blood spilled out of his head. The driver was watching us through the window. We waited for her to turn away. Then we jumped off our bikes and ran past Little Easy, over to the train station. From the stairwell, Alice was able to order us a ride home. We stayed hidden until the car pulled up.

Our new driver was a man in his late twenties with a British accent. I felt tense even as he navigated us toward my house. What if we couldn't get back home? What if we ended up on the bikes again? The radio was playing Primitive Radio Gods, "Standing Outside a Broken Phone Booth with Money in My Hand." Something about the old music was comforting. I reached for Hien's hand. Alice was fixing her hair, trying to smooth out the static electricity.

The driver picked up on our uneasiness. He passed us a basket of candy. Alice took a Crunch bar. I took a Butterfinger. Hien went for the licorice.

At the corner of Hoover and Beverly, he pulled out a tin. Soon I would be back to my life of illness: shuttling myself to doctors' appointments, getting IV infusions of experimental drugs. I savored my last minutes of health before I took the mint.

I CAME TO BY my front door. It was night, maybe a couple of hours later than when we had left, judging by the position of the moon. Hien and Alice were next to me. When we went inside, I found my husband passed out on the couch with a glass of whiskey in his hand. I took the whiskey from his fingers and placed the glass in the kitchen sink. Already I felt fatigued again. My chest got tight. Alice could tell I felt worse. She rubbed my back and told me they would find the right drugs for me soon.

She and Hien went home. Alfie was in the same navy fox pajamas I had dressed him in earlier that evening. He was sleeping with his pet lemon, which he carried all over our house from morning until night. I kissed his forehead, then started to get ready for bed. When I was changing into my pajamas, I noticed that I was still wearing the spin shoes. I unclipped them and tossed them to the side of the room. My skin smelled like sweat, but I would shower in the morning. I closed my eyes and slept seven hours, a gift.

I WOKE UP TO my husband having already cracked open the day. I could hear him making breakfast downstairs. He was trying to talk Alfie into a cheese omelet, but our son wasn't having it. Alfie was shouting for crackers and jelly instead.

He could yell for hours. He would always win. I lingered in bed for a few minutes with my phone. My son's screams made my bones hurt. Something about his cries turned my pain to ten. I was still exhausted despite the sleep. The disease knew how to take more than I could offer it. There was no replenishment.

Alice texted to ask if I was feeling okay. She suggested we meet up this weekend to discuss how to cancel the megalomaniac. I started to answer her but never sent my text. I went downstairs for a late breakfast. My husband was wobbly due to the lack of sleep. I felt bad seeing how tired my disease left him. He was the one who had to pick up the slack. I kissed him and my son. I wished I could be healthy for them.

LATER, I FOUND A tin of mints in my sweater pocket. Somehow I'd ended up with it after the ride home. I hid the tin in my desk. I couldn't let go of the dream of getting one more healthy day. Maybe if I took another mint, I would travel back as promised. The first trip had gone awry, but maybe the next one wouldn't.

I didn't tell my friends I had the mints. I knew they would think I was nuts, that I would get stuck on a bike and never come home again, that the megalomaniac would kill me for real this time—but there was no getting the idea out of my mind. I wanted to hike in the Dolomites, I wanted to swim with the penguins in South Africa, I wanted to hitchhike in Patagonia. I wanted to be anyone other than the mother with lupus who was too weak to care for her child.

While Alfie napped, I looked through Reddit to see if

anyone else had been sent to the future. No one else mentioned experiences that had gone awry. I started to believe our trip to the future was a fluke. Magical thinking, perhaps.

A few days later, while my husband took Alfie out on a hike, I took a mint. I closed my eyes and woke up in a different morning. My son popped his head in. He had grown at least a foot. He wanted to know if I would be driving him to football practice or if he was getting a ride with his father. "Go with your father," I told him. I had gone forward in time, but at least I wasn't on a bike. I still had almost an entire tin of mints in my possession; I figured I needed only one good one to go backward. I wasn't too worried. And I didn't feel sick.

I closed my eyes and took another mint, chewing it slowly this time. My husband popped into the bedroom. His forehead was wrinkled, and his brows were thick and gray. He said that Alfie needed me to buy him a mini-fridge for his dorm room.

"Dorm room?" I asked. "Why?"

My husband raised one of those brows. I gathered that Alfie was in college now. What about the meat of his life, the baseball games, the trips to national parks? I had missed his entire childhood. I felt less fatigued, but I couldn't feel happy about my health given that I had lost so much time with my son.

"You never cease to worry me," my husband said.

"I'll do better," I told him.

We watched television on the couch, but I couldn't pay attention. Some murder mystery, a dead girl dying for a second time. During commercial breaks, my husband quizzed me, concerned I had developed dementia.

"Who's the president?" he asked. "What did we eat for dinner last night? How old are you? How many fingers am I holding up?"

Finally, a question I could answer. Two fingers.

How could one mint rob me of so much life? I couldn't stay in this future. I wasn't sixty. I had to go back and reclaim my life.

I took another mint. This time, I wasn't set on going back to my pre-lupus time. Anytime earlier would do. I wanted to watch Alfie grow up. I wanted to see what it was like when he learned to speak in sentences. I wanted to know if he was a kind child. I wanted to know how his sense of humor had developed—if he liked puns like his father or deadpan humor like me. I wanted to know how long he carried around his pet lemon before he abandoned it for a flashier toy.

The next mint sent me fifteen years ahead. My son was married now. His wife worked as COO at a space start-up. They seemed well-off. They talked about helicopter trips to the moon and Greenland. I asked them what the moon was like. Dark, he said.

I took another mint. This time I woke up exhausted and brittle. Was I dead now? I felt dead. Every part of my body ached. It was a different kind of exhaustion from the one I was well-acquainted with: the exhaustion of old age.

Hien came over. Her face was covered in spots. She was wearing blue tights and a gray T-shirt dress. She said she had called another time-travel rideshare after our initial trip together, but she had been unlucky and had gotten stuck in the Peloton timeline. She'd passed most of her life on this bike powering Los Angeles. As a reward, they had given her several tins of mints to use in her retirement. She was still trying to find a way back home.

"They give you mints as incentives?" I asked.

She nodded.

"They're like lotto tickets," she said. "I have so many, I bet I have one of those backward mints."

"They were all supposed to be backward mints," I said.

I was starting to feel skeptical that any of ours were backward mints. How much time did I have left? What if the next mint finished me off? But I had already lost my entire life. There was no way out other than to take more mints.

This time I tried taking three mints instead of one. They took me back a few years, just when I started to gray. Six mints got me to Alfie's college years. I finished off the tin. This dose knocked me back to the original time, back when Alfie was a toddler, back into the pandemic, into the wildfires, the drought, the cusp of the electricity crisis. A time that had once seemed so difficult. Harold was walking around with secret-project dust in his hair, still pretending like he could hide his furniture from me.

Alfie curled up in my lap and gave me a kiss. He didn't know how to kiss yet and blew instead of smacking his lips. He was still holding his pet lemon. It was soft and bruised now. Every few days I had to replace it. I found lemons hidden all over our house, lemons he had rolled under beds or into the crawl space. They would decompose and become a part of our house. But a house wasn't meant to be clean. It was meant to bear the brunt of our lives. He giggled every time he found an old lemon.

There was no other place I wanted to be in this moment. But later, as I undressed for bed and the pain set in, I found another mint in my sweater pocket.

I kept the mint in my pocket and fingered it as I cycled through more lupus drugs. A year passed. Alfie grew older. He had his first soccer game coming up and I didn't have the strength to stand. He was starting to form memories of who I was. I wanted him to know me as a strong mom who could kick the ball around with him. Not the mom in bed. What if there was a way to time travel and bring my health back with me? I wanted to experience life as a healthy mom. There was nothing about my experience to suggest it was possible. But I couldn't let go of the dream. I took the mint.

THE SHARPEST KNIFE

It was my fault for not being careful when the disease started going around. I didn't take it seriously enough. No one in our friend group had come down with it. I'd read that some people got a cold. Some got no symptoms at all. Some people lost entire organs but always different ones. It sounded like a made-up disease, something concocted by trolls to mess with us. I couldn't tell the difference between fact and fiction now that the news was full of impersonators. We had been living in this mixed-up state for so long that I had forgotten what it was like to feel sure of something. I could believe whatever I wanted to believe. I wanted to believe it was safe to go to the Harry Styles concert.

It wasn't just my bad judgment at work.

"You deserve some fun," my husband agreed. "Get out of the house. Have a girls' night. The pandemic sounds made up."

I trusted Ralph's opinions. He was the smartest person I knew—an engineer at NASA's JPL. When I met him, he explained that he was living on Mars Time so he could monitor a rover he had sent there and he would have to live on Mars Time for the foreseeable future. On our first date, we had dinner for breakfast. He beamed as he explained to the waitress why he was eating steak at ten A.M. I fell in love with him right then.

Since Ralph was in the middle of his Mars workday, I went to the concert with my friend Sara. We sang until we were hoarse. It was just like we were sixteen again. Sara came down with a cold soon after the concert. A few weeks later, my heart had to be cut out of my chest. The surgeon explained that the way the disease worked, my heart was no longer compatible with my body; I would need to carry it around with me instead.

"Carry it?" I asked.

She nodded.

"Don't leave home without it," she warned. "It's still pumping your blood, but remotely now, by Bluetooth."

"I thought this was a fake disease," I said, terribly embarrassed. "I went to a concert. All those germs. Now I feel like an idiot."

"How could you know?" the surgeon sympathized. "Only fifty percent of the news is genuine. I wouldn't even say the genuine news is true, either, but at least it's not made up by some bored teenager."

"You can't trust the news," I said. "But if you don't read the news, you get sick."

"A conundrum," she agreed.

She stitched me up and sent me home with my heart inside one of those clear plastic belongings bags, handing it to me like a guppy I had won at the fair. I felt a bit woozy at first, but I was able to walk just fine, even carrying my heart in a bag.

"Did the surgery hurt?" Ralph asked, as he helped me into the car.

"Yeah," I told him.

It was the middle of the night on Mars, but he had stayed up to support me. He was a good husband.

I held the guppy heart on my lap as we drove. He white-knuckled it all the way home, stepping on the gas gently, as if my heart could fly out the window. I didn't have the bandwidth to manage his anxiety. I was trying to recover from surgery and was too busy pitying myself to comfort him. He was already a nervous driver, slamming his foot on the brake pedal anytime he caught a glimpse of a red light, and now I was entrusting him with the task of getting me home from the hospital with my heart no longer secured in my chest. I considered that maybe I should have asked someone calmer to drive us both, but we were already halfway home, and he was doing a good-enough job.

"So what now?" he asked. "You carry that bag around with you everywhere you go?"

"It's fine," I told him. "They said it has a range of fifty feet. I have to remember to bring it if I leave the house."

"Does it have an alarm or something?" he asked.

"You get too stressed out," I said, patting his knee. "Please remember to breathe."

I put on a calm front in front of my husband, but in truth, I didn't know how I was going to adjust. I was a jock. A gymnastics coach who dreamed of getting an athlete to the Olympics. I needed my heart. I couldn't lug it around in a belongings sack for the rest of my life. I spent a few weeks sitting on the couch in front of the television, too scared to venture out. My husband cooked our meals and cleaned. He was working hard to support me.

One evening, I discovered a show about one-armed lumberjacks who built log cabins in Washington.

"You should get up from the TV," he said, waving his arms around at me. "Maybe go for a walk. Get some fresh air. It will be good for you."

"Later," I replied. "I'm tired."

He told me I'd been convalescing for too long.

Normally I did handstands in between chores. I planked while I vacuumed under the couch. Now I was afraid to push my limits. There were implications for my career. It seemed unlikely I would be able to chase after gymnasts if I had to lug my heart around with me everywhere I went. My assistant, Fish, had taken over head-coaching duties while I recovered, but I was starting to see that I would never be well enough to coach again. This thought made me depressed. I didn't know who I was if not a coach or a jock.

I changed the TV channel and found a show about small people who made large airplanes. My evening then disappeared into this masterpiece.

"You need to get moving," my husband told me. "Develop some new routines," he added. "Ambulate. You'll feel better."

He said it was common to switch careers at my age. Maybe I would have gotten bored with trying to get a gymnast to the Olympics. He said when he met me I had many dreams, but I couldn't remember any of them. He was trying his best to cheer me up.

"Am I lost?" I asked him.

He shook his head, but I could tell he thought I was.

There were plenty of shows to keep me busy, now that I had this big hole in my life. I watched a show about ponies who painted houses on the weekends. At least my illness had coincided with the golden age of television.

AFTER A FEW MONTHS of feeling sorry for myself, I was finally ready to venture out of the house. I was sick of looking at my heart in its sad little belongings bag. Now that people would see it, I wanted an upgrade. I ended up putting my heart in a mason jar. I had many lying around from when we made our own jam. I went to the farmers market and strolled around with the jar in the crook of my arm as I shopped for fresh eggs. My genius husband was right—it was nice to get out of the house, to feel the light on my face again. It was so sunny in California, I could improve my mood just by going outside.

I made it a goal to take a long walk every day. I started to forget that my heart was not in my chest. I got used to lugging it around with me. I excelled at it, even. People complimented my cute jar. I fought my way back to health and found enjoyment in the challenge of learning how to be fit as a sick person. I learned to hike with my mason-jar heart. I learned how to do burpees over it. It felt good to get some endorphins, to feel my body working as it should. I lugged the heart up to the park helipad and posed in a handstand with the jar on the ground next to me. People I knew were starting to lose organs, and I wanted them to know you could bounce back. The more photos I posted of myself exercising with my heart, the more likes I got.

I MUST HAVE RADIATED joy in my photos, because strangers started to message me their stories. People said I was brave for displaying my heart in a jar, for not letting the disease bring me down. The fame came quick. I got thirty-three thousand likes the time I wore the sweater with the heart pattern stitched in, cradling my real heart front and center in my arms. Sixty-six thousand when I did push-ups over the mason jar during golden hour. Kids started carrying around fake hearts in mason jars in solidarity. The last thing I expected was to become an influencer, but that's what happened.

Sometimes I paired my photos with quotes from my favorite books, even if they didn't make sense. I discovered the captions needed the right cadence more than they needed to convey a specific meaning. Crafting a good social-media profile was hard work. It was a full-time job. I put a lot of effort into it.

Companies sent me their cookware, their self-help books, their pressed juices to promote. I was courted by athletic-apparel brands, even though I was no longer an athlete or a coach. Who needed the real Olympics? My own Olympics were happening right outside my house, in the park where I exercised with my heart.

JUST AS I WAS getting into my stride on social media, Ralph got the disease. His illness came for his brain. The doctors said they were going to have to remove it soon, but he kept delaying the procedure.

"Why did it have to be my brain?" he asked. "It couldn't have affected my liver instead?"

"I'm sure you'll be just as smart without it," I assured him. I didn't know if he would be smart anymore, but I wanted to repay the favor by comforting him after he had been there for me.

After the surgery, I drove him home from the hospital carefully. I didn't want to get into a fender bender and knock Ralph's brain onto the floor. I would never be able to forgive myself if his brain split apart because of me.

"Don't worry, we'll get through this," I told him.

He nodded but didn't seem so sure.

Our mason jars were too small for his brain, so I took him to the hardware store to find one that was large enough to accommodate him. I tried to make it fun. I made sure to give him compliments. I told him it would be cool that people could see that he had an extra-large brain. He wouldn't have to talk about his job to sound smart. Everyone would be able to see exactly how smart he was, because his huge brain would be right there in front of him. He smiled a little bit. I always knew how to make him feel better. He was extra affectionate all night.

Then, a few weeks later, he lost his Mars rover. He said that he couldn't remember where he'd sent it. When NASA fired him, he flipped our kitchen table. The loss of his career sent him into despair.

"I'm dumb now," he shouted. "I was a sharp person. It was my whole identity. This is my worst nightmare."

"You are still very smart even without your brain," I reassured him. "Everyone makes mistakes."

He decided to stay on Mars Time even though he would no longer be going into work. He said it was important to keep the same life rhythms. I didn't protest. I could see him coming unraveled and I wanted to keep clear of this mess. He parked himself in front of the television for the next few weeks. He said television was the only thing that made him feel better.

"Remember when you said I was watching too much television?" I asked. "You could use your own advice."

He shrugged.

I hated to see my husband struggling. I gently suggested I could be an inspiration to him since I, too, had recently lost my career and had embraced a new identity as an influencer. "Look at how I'm living my life," I said. "I'm stronger than ever without my heart. I go on so many hikes. You'll find a way to be smart again. You just have to believe in yourself."

I pulled up some of my inspirational posts and showed them to him.

Don't let fear hold you back, one read. Another said, *Live in the now. Be your best self.*

"You never used to talk like that," Ralph complained.

"Well, now I need to be optimistic," I said, hurt. "And it's working. Look at my likes."

"Are you letting your success get to your head?" Ralph wondered aloud.

"I don't think so," I said.

I dragged him back out into the world, one brunch at a time. Once he got used to going out, he remembered how much he liked being somewhere other than our couch. Suddenly he was out all the time. I was glad to see him cheerier, but we had a new set of problems. He had become forgetful—always jumping into the car without his brain jar. He got into several accidents that sent our premiums skyrocketing. He used to be a careful driver. He'd never been in an accident before.

I reminded him that all he had to do was remember to carry his jar around and life would be fine, but he asked how he was supposed to remember his jar without his brain. I told him he'd get the hang of it soon and wrote a reminder on the back of his hand, but the message didn't help. Then he said it was easier for me. I still had my brain and I didn't even need one. He was being rude, but I understood he was in crisis, so I gave him some grace.

One day, while Ralph was fretting about his lost salary, I showed him my deposits from a leggings company.

"You don't have to worry," I told him. "We'll be okay without your job. I can be the breadwinner now."

I told him that every time I posted a photo of myself, I got paid. A photo of me in the splits with the heart held triumphantly over my head had made us millionaires.

"Now I feel useless," he said.

I'd thought the sight of the money in my bank account

would reassure him, but he only looked more stressed out at the idea of losing his job. He liked being the one to make money. But I was happier now than I had ever been.

MY SISTER CAUGHT THE disease next. It came for her uterus. A uterus was tougher to carry around. It wasn't a cute accessory. It didn't have much of a shape. It wouldn't fit in a mason jar either. It fell flat like a jellyfish once they took it out. She decided to keep it in a trash bag slung over her shoulder. She said she was going to lean into her suffering. She'd already had a miserable life anyway. She was in a biochemistry PhD program, but she'd lost interest in completing her degree now that real scientists were indistinguishable from fake ones.

I told her I didn't think anyone should lean into suffering, but she disagreed.

"Why couldn't it have been a gallbladder or another useless organ?" she asked. Then she looked at me accusingly. "You should have been the one to lose your uterus."

"Me?" I asked, shocked.

She nodded.

"You didn't even want children," she said. "You don't need yours."

"I lost my heart," I said. "I needed that."

"But you're doing better without it," she complained.

"You think this life came easily?" I asked. "I had to work for it. But look at where I am now. I'm so happy."

She frowned.

My sister had been weird ever since we were kids. I knew

she felt like she couldn't keep up. It wasn't my fault that I was more popular in high school. I was a friendly person who complimented people. She rolled her eyes whenever anyone talked to her. She wore smelly clothes to repel people. Back then I ended up ignoring her whenever we ran into each other. Maybe I could have mentored her or included her socially, but that only occurred to me later, as an adult.

"You've always treated me like I'm stupid and lucky," I told her. "You said I was dumb for going to the Harry Styles concert. And now look at you. You're sick too. I guess you're not so smart."

"I got it at the grocery store," she said, offended. "I hardly left my house."

"You went on dates too," I said.

She frowned.

"I had to," she said. "I'm single. I can't hole up for the rest of my life. How else would I meet someone before my eggs dry up?"

"I guess we're equally stupid, then," I shouted. "Admit it! We're equally stupid. Say it!"

She looked away. She refused to admit she was just as stupid as me. She was a bit like Ralph. Always had to be the smarter one.

She declined over the next few months. She wouldn't answer texts, which forced me to drive to her apartment. There I found her bins overflowing with trash. She'd been wearing the same pajamas for weeks. I could tell by the smell. I had to help her snap out of her funk. I figured it was a sign of growth on my part to recognize I could have a positive influence on her. She refused to use social media, so I printed out my most popular posts and taped them to her apartment walls, hoping they would inspire her. Maybe I was a mean big sister when I was younger, but I really cared for her now.

I still had a gymnastics coach inside me. I designed workouts and drills to get her moving. I made her do high knees and squats. I made her do wood chops. "We're going to turn your life around," I said. "We're going to fight this."

"I don't want to fight," she said. "And anyway, you're only doing this for you. I make you feel useful. You can't coach gymnastics anymore, so you only have me to boss around."

She still knew just how to hurt me.

"I want to help you," I said. "It hurts to see you depressed."

She didn't seem to believe me, but I was telling the truth.

A FEW MONTHS LATER, Ralph started to have seizures. The first time I walked in on him twitching on the ground, I was scared. But he had a smile on his face. He said he was in outer space while he was seizing. It started to happen so often that he was rarely not in outer space. He came back talking about a freeze-dried ice cream pop-up bar he claimed to have found on the moon. He said that the ice cream up there tasted unreal.

"Is this the disease talking?" he asked.

"You shouldn't be getting seizures," I said. "You don't even have a brain."

"It doesn't make sense," he agreed. "Shouldn't the mason jar be getting the seizures?"

I pulled out my phone to do some research. The scientists or "scientists" were saying the disease could give you seizures now, even if your brain was out. But it could also give you a heart attack or a very long panic attack or make you crawl everywhere or walk super slow. It could turn you into a robot.

"I don't want to walk super slow," my husband said, in a shaky voice. "I'm a fast walker. Always have been."

It was true that his fast-walking was one of his best qualities. As a gymnastics coach, I walked fast too. I estimated this mutual fast-walking gave us an extra 20 percent of life that other people didn't get. But maybe it wasn't true that this disease caused slow-walking. Why should it?

"We don't know what's real," I reminded him. "This information is probably nonsense from teenagers impersonating scientists."

He crawled to the bathroom. The next day, he walked in slow motion.

"I'm turning into a robot," he whimpered.

His hands were trembling. I told him he was being a hypochondriac.

"No I'm not," he said. "I can't walk fast anymore."

He lifted his leg to show me. His knee got stuck up high. He needed my help to push it back to the ground.

"Hmm," I said, squinting at him. "You don't look like a robot. Can you close your eyes and relax your muscles? Like, do a full body scan. Make sure you get every tendon. Really release it."

"Is this a nervous breakdown?" he asked.

"It could be," I told him.

"Does the disease make you cold?" he asked, shivering. "Does it make you sadder than you've ever been? I hope it is the disease. If it's not the disease, then it's just life. But I don't want it to be life. I want it to be the disease, something separate from myself, something that can be cured. They're going to find a cure for being a robot. I know it. They're probably already working on it."

He tried to take another step, but his leg got stuck in the air again.

"See?" he cried out, frightened. "What's going to happen to me?"

"Massage your temples," I told him. "Now picture yourself moving with ease. Visualize your next step."

He did what I said.

"It didn't work," he said, opening his eyes again. "I'm still stuck."

"Stay off the internet," I said. "Tomorrow you'll forget someone said you could turn into a robot." I didn't know for sure staying off the internet would be enough, but I was hopeful.

"I just want to be myself again," he said.

"You will be," I assured him.

He asked me to walk him to the bed. He said his legs needed oil. He fell asleep quickly, thank goodness. I needed to get back to work. I hadn't posted in twenty-four hours. My followers probably thought something bad had happened to me. My fans were overinvolved. I didn't want them to call in a welfare check. I selected a few photographs to post from my recent shoot. *Another helipad workout in the books! Living my best pandemic life,* I wrote. It briefly made me feel good to see that people admired me. I looked strong in my photos. By the time I finished editing my next set of posts, my husband was snoring loudly next to me.

IN THE MORNING, I was the first to get up. I went to wash my face and brush my teeth. When I returned to the bedroom, Ralph asked me to boot him up.

"Turn me on!" he barked.

"Really?" I asked.

"You have to find the power switch," he said. "I don't know where it is."

I scanned his back for a switch and pushed on a spot that seemed like a place where someone would put a robot switch.

"My legs are rusting up," he said. "Can you bring me breakfast?"

I made him toast and cheesy eggs. He talked about his symptoms while he ate. His arms seemed to be working fine. I wanted to listen, but I needed to detach from his anxiety. It was harder to deal with his problems than my sister's. His bad mood was bringing me down. It had taken all my strength to not let the surgery ruin my life and I was proud of myself for moving on, but I needed to control my environment by keeping a positive spin on the illness. I was starting to resent my husband for not keeping his anxiety in check. Seeing as we were married, his bad vibes were rubbing off on me. I told him that if he was going to continue to be a robot, I could no longer support him and would need to take a break. I had to protect myself.

"But I helped you recover from heart surgery," he said. "I brought you food for a month. I was your cheerleader."

"And I helped you recover from brain surgery," I told him. "This is different."

"I don't think it is different," he said.

"You refuse to get better," I said. "You should be fine by now."

I ran errands to distract myself. I went to get my nails done. When I came back home, he was frozen in the same spot where I had left him.

"Turn me back on," he said. "My switch is off again."

"How can your switch be off if you're talking?" I asked.

"I don't know," he said. "But it's off. I can tell. Will you switch it on?"

I flipped the switch.

A FEW WEEKS PASSED with no improvement. I spent as much time out of the house as I could, trying to take my mind off things. Ralph complained that he wanted to go with me, but I told him I couldn't carry him plus my heart and his brain. I told him he would have to walk himself if he wanted to come.

"Not fair," he cried. "I can't walk in this condition!"

"Give it a shot," I said. "You might feel better."

I guess I was hoping he would snap out of it. He was able to move his leg a bit but then fell to the ground. I didn't help him stand up.

"You're a selfish person," he said. "You only care about how many likes you get."

"You've misunderstood," I told him. "Likes pay bills. You should be happy we are rich. I'm happy!"

"You don't look happy," Ralph said. This was true.

"It is hard work being happy," I said.

I went out to brunch with Sara and left him behind. Maybe it was shitty of me, but I needed to get out of the house. It was good to see a friend.

ONE DAY, A FEW months later, Ralph asked for a divorce while beeping and booping in the kitchen. He said my lack of support was a deal-breaker. He needed more from a wife. I was too shocked to defend myself. What about my mental state? Did it matter how much I'd been through? He was angry at me. Nothing had prepared me for how fast our marriage could deteriorate. We'd been content before either of us got sick, but the pandemic had ruined everything. He had even gotten a lawyer. I recognized the name from a bench billboard—someone who normally dealt with asbestos suits. Still, he was good at his job. Better than my lawyer. Ralph couldn't work without his brain, so the lawyer negotiated for me to pay his expenses until he got his brain situation sorted out.

Ralph got a one-bedroom apartment down the hill, with an art deco kitchen. The apartment was walking distance to the cute shops on Sunset we used to visit when we were dating. He paid for a robot minder, someone to keep his gaskets clean and his joints oiled.

I missed our fast walks. I missed holding his hand as we watched the show about the people who ate toilet paper. And I felt guilty for being a bad wife. For deciding my mental health was more important than his.

* * *

THE ROBOT MINDER WAS busy peeling Ralph's fruit when I came to visit. The oranges and pears sat in a pile on a tray, the peels left by the sink. She was young, maybe twenty-two, a bit caustic. Thought she knew everything. Immediately got under my skin. He wouldn't talk to me, so I was forced to interact with her.

"He's such a kind man," she told me, as I walked in. "He tips well."

"It's my money," I told her. "I tip well."

She ran her fingers through her thick curls.

"Not like it's hard work, though, is it?" she said. "You put on yoga pants, take a photo, and people dump money into your bank account. I'd love to have a job like that. I break my back moving this guy around. You know how heavy he is?"

She seemed to be irritating me on purpose. "You're paid to enable," I told her. "You're not a wife, and you'll never be his."

I couldn't tell if Ralph enjoyed my visits. Before he moved out, I had never seen him aloof. He was an emotional person—too emotional, even. Maybe he didn't care about me anymore. Maybe he was enjoying my money without me. Maybe all he ever wanted was a minder and not a wife. If we were a good couple, wouldn't we have been able to support each other in sickness and in health? My mind went to a dark place, but then I saw him wiggle his eyebrow at me in a quiet moment when his minder was dumping out his bedpan. I loved the way his eyebrows wiggled. It was an involuntary reaction whenever I said something funny or wore a dress that showed some leg. I smiled. He still loved me.

There was a chance I could win him back if I tried hard enough.

I kept coming by after my photo shoots. I felt lucky my career was continuing to take off. I needed the likes to distract me from the sadness I felt when Ralph didn't answer me. I returned to the app often to see them pile up. But even with hundreds of thousands of hearts lighting up, something was missing.

FOR HIS FORTIETH BIRTHDAY, I got him a bottle of Suntory whiskey and a soft-looking yellow cashmere sweater. I figured robots were cold, all that metal. It seemed like a thoughtful gift. He handed the minder the bottle of whiskey and asked her if she could clean him with it later. He told me it had been a long time since he felt cold or hot or any other sensation, so a sweater wasn't needed.

"It's just a gesture, then," I said. "Just say thank you and accept the gift."

"I don't accept the gift," he said. At least he was speaking to me now. This felt like progress.

He told the minder to lubricate his elbows so he could cross his arms. He told the minder to turn his head to the left, so he could be petulant. She did as she was told.

"You don't have to visit," he told me.

"I want to visit," I said. "I live up the street. You're on my way home from the park. It's convenient. Plus, I miss you."

"I don't miss you," he said. "If I'm going to be alone, I may as well actually be alone."

He told the minder to push him to the window so he

could look at the police helicopter hovering overhead. I folded up the sweater and left it on the kitchen counter.

I WENT OVER TO my sister's house to check on her. She said she was doing better. I didn't force her to act cheery or take pictures of her path to recovery. I brought her some food and unloaded her groceries. She seemed grateful once she knew I wasn't going to make her perform.

She listened to my problems. I had a lot to say about Ralph. She said he probably just needed some time to adjust. He'd been smart his whole life and was facing an identity crisis not so different from my own. It was bound to make him neurotic. I reminded her that I easily overcame my identity crisis. She said he would overcome his, too, if I gave him enough time. She agreed the eyebrow wiggle was significant.

Now that Ralph and I were having problems, I was finally experiencing the kind of sisterly relationship I had craved. This was the kind of relationship sisters had on those television programs I liked to watch.

A few days later, she sent me a news article that seemed true and could help fix Ralph. She was a real scientist. I trusted her links. I went by his place. His minder walked out of the living room just as soon as I walked in. She had dressed him in a sweater but not the one I gave him.

"How are you doing?" I asked Ralph.

"Same," he said. "Robot is always same."

I set my hand on his. He didn't protest.

"Well, I have some good news," I said.

He seemed interested. A good sign. I pulled out my phone and read him the article.

"*After conducting several studies, scientists in Switzerland have fully determined that the disease does not cause roboticism,*" I read. "*The earlier reports were mistaken.*"

"Oh yeah?" he asked, perking up.

"So whatever is happening to you has nothing to do with the disease," I said. "You are not a robot. You might be a little stiff. Maybe you have arthritis?"

The minder by then had reentered the room and was hovering next to him, ready to adjust his cheeks into an appropriate expression.

"How do we know you didn't make up this news?" she asked me, crossing her arms.

I resented her for putting her own financial needs ahead of Ralph's mental health.

"Do you trust me?" I asked him.

He thought about it, then took a step by himself, then another one.

"See, you're human," I told him. "No robots here."

"I guess I *am* human," he said, confused. "What now?" he wondered aloud. "Being a robot was kind of my thing. Now I don't have a thing. I'm just an ordinary guy who is missing his brain."

"You can come over sometime if you want," I told him. "Don't be shy."

HE CAME BY FOR a date on Friday. He was wearing the sweater I bought him. I was thrilled. I brought out a case of Pliny the Elder and cooked a real dinner, with vegetables and everything. This was the beginning of my long apology to him. He said he appreciated the support.

We watched a show about weird jobs. This episode featured the world's sharpest knife and the people who spent their time sharpening it. The sharpeners hardly had time to themselves. All they did was work to keep this knife sharp. What a sacrifice. We heard from their families and friends in the interview.

"I haven't seen Ken since he got this job," his brother said. "I really miss him. We used to do everything together. Our bowling team hasn't won a tournament since Ken began to sharpen this knife."

"The cost of weird jobs," my husband said, in sync with the narrator.

He could always predict what the narrator would say. He was still smart.

"I've missed you," I said.

"I missed you too," he said, resting his head against my shoulder. I felt relaxed sitting with him in front of the TV. We'd had a terrible couple of years, but television would heal us. It was our medicine. I left my phone on the table, even though I'd yet to check the likes on my latest post. I didn't need to know how much money I was making just then. I wanted to be present. We would never be able to have the life we originally imagined, but we would be fine if we had each other.

Ralph's brain was sitting on the end table, next to my heart. Two mason jars side by side, right where they belonged.

SVEN

Someone has left an earpiece on a park bench, which I spot during my morning walk. There is a tiny voice coming through the speaker. I put the earpiece in my ear so I can hear. A man's voice says, *Now walk over to the woman in the blue hat and tell her you're addicted to sex. Then go over to the bald man and punch him in the stomach.*

"I'm not going to do that," I say.

The man pauses.

Who are you? Where is Sven?

"I don't know," I say. "I think he left."

I look around for someone who looks like a Sven, but I don't see anyone like that nearby. Then I spot a turtlenecked guy getting into his car on the street. Maybe a Sven. I hurry over, just making it before he backs out of his spot. I wave at him. He stares at me like I am weird for following him.

"Did you forget your earpiece?" I ask, pointing at my ear.

He shakes his head vigorously.

"Okay, then," I say, backing away. "Have a nice day, I guess."

The turtlenecked man drives away quickly.

"I can't find Sven," I say to the man in the ear.

Can you help me? the man in the ear asks. *I'll get fired if I lose him.*

He sounds agitated. I have a few hours free, so I figure, why not help him? I have nowhere to be, no one at home waiting for me. I can look for Sven as I walk. I cut through a pack of women in buttery yoga pants on my way back to the path. They seem annoyed that I am walking so close to them, but they are six wide, taking up the whole sidewalk, and it's not my fault I have to get through. I continue around the lake on the clockwise loop, just as I would have if I had never found the earpiece.

"It would help if you described him," I tell him. I don't know who I'm looking for here. The man in the ear says I've made a good point, but he struggles to find a useful description.

Oh, uh, let me think. He's tall. . . . He looks like a Ken doll, except he's sad. A little unstable, actually. Right now he's really upset about a zit on his chin.

I glance around for someone who fits that description.

I'm so boned, the man frets. *I have a wife and two kids. Do you know how expensive preschool is? I can't lose my job.*

"I'll find him," I assure him. "You work with Sven?"

He works for me, the guy says. *He's the talent.*

I don't know what to say. This is about as far as I can get in a conversation that is not held over text. Still, it feels nice to talk to this man. It's been a while since I've talked to anyone.

I need to jump on a call and figure this out, the man says. *Don't go anywhere, okay?*

"Be right here," I say. He puts on some wait music. I recognize the riff. "Zero," by the Smashing Pumpkins, a song I haven't heard in a while.

I stopped listening to music after my friend Nola was hit by a truck while on a run. She was wearing headphones and couldn't hear it approach. I met her on a message board for a band we both liked. We used to follow our favorite bands all over the West Coast. We were like a married couple who never made out. She understood my weird parts. She didn't care that I was shy. I'd never met anyone who was comfortable with silence before her. That was ten years ago, but I still miss her.

I don't hear from the man in the ear by the time I'm finished walking, so I go home and eat dinner in front of my computer. I DM someone named Nikita. He's a truck driver from Spokane. He styles his hair in a pompadour, likes the Smiths, says he's twenty-six.

What U wearing, Nikita texts.

Just undies, I tell him, though I am wearing gold velour sweats. I take a bite of a burrito as I text Nikita. A bolt of pain shoots up a nerve, but it's gone before I can be mad. It's my fault for not getting that tooth fixed. Then the man in the ear comes back on, so I tell Nikita I'll chat with him later.

Sven?

"Still me," I say. "Sorry to disappoint. But you haven't been fired yet."

Not yet, he agrees.

"Why do you need Sven?" I ask.

I'm a producer, he says. *I'm making a TV show.*

"About Sven?"

Obviously we'll have to pivot, he says. *You game?*

After giving it some thought, I tell him I'll do it. I've always wanted to be on television. To have people know me. Maybe it seems like a shortcut for making friends. I warn the man in the ear that I get self-conscious when I'm photographed. He tells me I won't have to worry—the cameras will be hidden. He will make it as painless for me as possible. We agree to start work in the morning. I keep the earpiece in while I sleep in case he needs anything.

THE MAN IN THE ear wakes me up at five A.M. I'm annoyed at first and cuss him out, but then I remember I am going to be on television. I ask him how I should dress. He tells me to dress like myself. This is a show about me. "Makes sense," I tell him.

And hurry, he says. *You're late. The crew is in place.*

I go with my usual face, no makeup, then search my closet for clothes. I decide on a sleeveless T-shirt and Adidas exercise shorts. I ask where we're going. He says I should do whatever I'd normally do. I tell him I need to do deliveries. Rent's due soon. He says that's perfect—they've already installed hidden cameras in my car so they can film me as I work.

I get in the car and accept my first job of the day. I don't feel like I'm on a TV show. As I drive away from my apartment building, the man in the ear asks me questions. He wants me to talk about how I ended up with a job doing deliveries. He says we will be doing many of these on-the-fly interviews. *Just talk naturally,* he says. *Don't overthink it.*

I try my best, even though I feel like I'm talking to myself. I tell him I started driving maybe four years ago. I was working at a juice shop and didn't enjoy dealing with customers. I was fired for throwing an orange across the courtyard after a customer was condescending. I didn't throw the orange at the customer, but it was still an issue with management.

Do you like your job now? he asks.

No one has ever asked me such a probing question before. I pull over so I can think about how to answer. He tells me to drive as I talk. They can't cut to footage of me in a parked car when I'm supposed to be driving. I pull back into the street and answer the question.

"I like that it allows me to work as much as needed," I say. "There's always another job, another person who needs a sandwich." I take jobs in different parts of town to keep it fresh. Some days I go out as far as Riverside or Long Beach. Once, I went up to Santa Barbara and delivered a pizza to someone on the beach. It brightens my mood to see nice places.

AFTER WE FINISH THE interview, I stop by a California Pizza Kitchen and drive a salad and Sprite out to a six-story apartment building in Santa Monica. The man in the ear asks me to drop off the salad several times so they can get close-ups of my hands. I notice then that my cuticles are cracked, the skin is peeling, and my nails are slightly yellow. Now that I'm going to be on TV, I'll have to take better care of myself.

After I complete a few more jobs, the man in the ear tells me to drive to my mother's house.

"I don't usually talk to her," I tell him, caught off guard.

That's why we're doing it, he says. *This is a show about a complex mother–daughter relationship. It's a story about inherited trauma, intergenerational pain as told by the daughter of an immigrant.*

"I wanted to do a comedy," I say.

Some parts will be funny, he tells me.

I drive out to Santa Ana, where my mother lives. On the way, I hang a new air freshener in the car. I keep a stash of paper ones from the convenience store. They are my happy place. I need to be in my happy place if I'm going to see my mother. She lives far enough away that I can usually pretend she doesn't exist. I try to remember the last time we talked. Maybe her fiftieth. She'd thrown herself a party. I brought her presents, doing my duty as a good Thai daughter, even though we don't talk much.

She answers the door in her robe, braless, barefoot, with pink toenails, her hair clipped out of her face like she's in the middle of getting a haircut. She seems surprised to see me. I tell her I was working nearby.

I follow her through the door, but the house isn't ours on the inside. I grew up in a two-bedroom house built in the fifties. The furniture should have been mismatched. The coffee table should have been covered with stains from our mugs. But the house I enter is built more recently, with modern furniture, no coffee rings. Someone has decorated this living room with rugs, plants, and throw pillows.

"Where am I?" I ask.

We rented a prop house, the man in the ear explains.

"Why?"

It's not important, he says.

"But you're using the real façade," I say, trying to make sense of this. "I walked through my real front door to get into the prop house."

My mother wants to know who I am talking to and why her house looks different. I tell her we are doing a show. The man in the ear interrupts and says he will fill her in later. He wants me to talk naturally, to get back into the scene. I reach into an open bag of potato chips on a nearby table and bring several to my mouth. I can tell my mother is ready to launch into criticism. I recognize the windup. Her mouth curves a bit before she gives unwanted advice. My body clenches in preparation.

"Should you be eating that?" she asks. "It's fattening."

I put the chips down.

"You came just in time for breakfast," she says.

"Actually, I'm not hungry," I say.

"Eggs are good food," she says. "Better than potato chips. They won't make your skin break out."

"I need a minute," I say. I walk outside to get some air.

My mother worked two jobs when I was a child. I was left to look after my younger sister, Suzi, and make sure she was fed. I'm not angry about that part. She needed to pay the bills and I did fine. What I hate is the constant criticism.

Let's try it again, the man in the ear says. *Only this time, don't stay guarded. Tell her how you feel when she criticizes you.*

"It's hard," I tell him.

It's not supposed to be easy, he says.

I start the scene back in the car and then walk up to my old house. This time I notice the roses out front. The bushes look healthy. My mother opens the door, looking just as surprised as she was the first time. I didn't know she could act.

"I missed you, D," she says. "Why are you here? Are you hungry? Do you need money?"

"No, I have tons," I say, following her in again.

I take a seat on the clean, overstuffed couch that isn't ours. Even though this is the second time running the scene, it feels wrong to sit on a couch without ketchup stains. The couch was stained because a child (me) was busy being the mother while the mother was out of the house. I served dinner to my sister on the couch. I make a note to tell the man in the ear that the couch is an important part of the story. I want to do the scene again after they swap it in.

But then thinking of the couch makes me sad. It makes me think of how I rarely hear from Suzi. She lives in New York. She is a lawyer now. She doesn't call me, even though I raised her. She talks to my mother. She never says a bad word about her, I suspect due to the habits ingrained from our culture. We respect our elders no matter how they treat us.

I have memories of my mother sending money back to Bangkok whenever she had extra to spare. Whatever happened between her and our grandmother loomed over our own childhoods, but we were never privy to the details. We only saw how my mother got quiet when we asked her questions about her life in Bangkok. We gathered that Grandma had gotten into some messed-up stuff. We wouldn't have known from our trips back to Thailand, when my mother would bring her suitcases full of American purses and lotions and free makeup samples. Maybe if they'd had screaming matches, we would have understood who we were. That we were going to keep people at a distance to avoid having our worst qualities pointed out to us. Even Suzi doesn't get into relationships, though she acts like she knows everything.

"How've you been?" I ask my mother.

"I thought you were mad at me," she says.

"I don't want to fight," I tell her.

"You haven't answered the phone for months," she says.

"I've been working a lot," I say. "Are you still seeing the same three boyfriends?"

"Which ones?" she asks. She juggles many men. It's a point of pride for her. She likes the company but doesn't want anyone to get too close.

"You waste your life texting weirdos," she says.

"You've misunderstood," I tell her. "I'm the weirdo."

You're getting to it too soon, the man interrupts. *The conversation doesn't seem natural. Chitchat about normal stuff. There was the bit with the potato chips. That was a real slice of life.*

"Sorry," I say.

I scroll through DMs, trying to work up the nerve to start the scene again, when my mother rips the phone from my hands and flicks it away. It bounces off the edge of the counter and lands face down on the hard tile floor. When I pick it up,

I see that the glass has cracked. The screen is now filled with black and white lines. Resetting the phone does nothing. It doesn't hurt her to see me upset. I am usually a calm person, but she knows how to press my only button.

Great stuff, the man in the earpiece says. *But we didn't get your reaction. We need to do it again.*

"I'm going home," I tell him.

I don't know how to live without a phone. My hands don't know what to hold. I wish I had worn shorts with pockets. I have nowhere to stuff them. They dangle uselessly from the ends of my arms.

I jump into my car and speed away from the house, feeling sick. The stuff I repress starts to come floating up my esophagus. There is a burning in my chest. I try to press on the part that hurts, but I can't find it. The pain moves to my armpit. I've never experienced a mental-health crisis before. Either that, or I've always been experiencing one and I don't know what it feels like to not be in crisis.

"Why did you make me go back inside?" I ask the man in the ear. "I don't like being emotional. I like being chill. I have my shit together. But not when I'm around her."

The real you isn't chill, he tells me. *I'm thinking your issues can be traced back to your alcoholic grandmother in Thailand. Perhaps you and your mother need to confront her together.*

"I don't think I'm ready for that," I tell him. I pull over when I see a Best Buy. My hands shake as I wait for my turn. There are other people here with cracked phones. They stroll through the flat-screen TV aisles, waiting to be called. How are they so calm? Sweat is pouring out of me. My lips don't know how to make words. My fingers tap into the air as if

I'm typing. Finally it's my turn. The technician tells me he will do his best to transfer my data to the new phone.

"*Data* is a weird name for it," I tell the technician. "I think of it more as friends?"

That's a good line, the man in the ear says to himself. I can almost hear him circling my words on a piece of paper.

I sleep cradling my new phone. Nikita sends me cute texts all morning, lots of heart emojis. He says he missed me while I was offline. I stay in bed chatting with him.

The man in the ear isn't too happy about how late it is getting. He spends the rest of the morning coaxing me into the car. He wants to film more scenes in Santa Ana. I protest, but he says I don't have to talk to my mom. He wants to get footage of me driving through my old neighborhood, in front of my high school. He says it's important to give people a full picture of who I am.

I pick up a few delivery jobs as I make my way down. The bad feelings start to come back up my esophagus well before I exit the freeway. It was a mistake coming here.

We drive by my old haunts. He asks me to talk about my high school and what life was like back there. I tell him I spent those years dreaming of moving up to Los Angeles, where I would start a new life, maybe as a comedian. I saved up enough money to rent a studio apartment in a cheap part of East Hollywood. I had imagined that once I moved, I would become an interesting person.

Once he says we have enough footage, I tell the man in the ear that we're going to try something new today. I'm going to order him around. He chuckles, uncomfortable.

What do you have in mind? he asks.

"Go to your brother's house and confess you slept with

his wife. Tell him about your pot addiction. And your porn addiction too."

You think this is funny, bossing me around, the man in the ear says.

"It's hilarious," I tell him.

He pretends to tell his wife about me, as if I can't hear. *I know this crazy girl in Hollywood,* he says. I snort.

I can't remember the last time I've had this much fun. As I drive home, he tells me about his family. He says he met his wife on the show where strangers talk through a barn door. After they got married, the host slid open the door and their bodies were revealed. Melissa was just as beautiful as he'd imagined. He knew he'd chosen correctly as soon as the barn door opened.

I feel jealous as he tells me how much he loves his wife. It's like my whole life is conducted behind a barn door. No one sees my face. They see the masks I choose. Maybe one day that barn door will slide open for me, too, and there will be someone on the other side who loves me.

When I arrive in Los Angeles, I pick up two dozen donuts and several milkshakes from the vegan shop and drop them off at a new construction house in Boyle Heights.

IN THE MORNING I lie in bed talking to the man in the ear instead of texting Nikita. He asks about my dreams for the future. I tell him I'm saving up money to visit Kauai. On Sundays I work two extra hours to put money toward that fund.

Why Kauai?

"Looks nice," I tell him. He senses I am holding back.

He's right. I tell him about Nola. The last time I saw her, she'd just returned from a trip there with her parents. She stayed at one of those resorts with two waterslides and a lazy river. She had never felt more relaxed. I told her I wanted to go back there with her. We went on hikes in the Angeles to prepare for the Nā Pali Coast. That was the closest I came to acknowledging my feelings for her. She died before we could make a plan.

It sounds like your relationship with your mother is holding you back from connecting with people, he says.

"Maybe," I tell him. "But I need more time."

Don't worry, he says. *We have a few weeks to work through this together.*

"What would I do without you?" I ask, genuinely curious.

LATER, MY MOTHER SHOWS up unexpectedly. I don't know why she's here. She's never seen my apartment before. She prefers that I visit her house. She seems shocked by how little I have.

"Are you poor?" she asks.

"No," I say.

"Are you sure?" she says. I don't answer this time. I haven't gotten around to putting up decorations. White walls are calming to me. Maybe I think of every place as temporary. I am still waiting for my real life to begin. It's a life I can't yet picture, but I am running out of time to come up with a vision. Moving to Hollywood wasn't enough to get my life started. I have yet to take a real step forward. But this show is a start. I want to do a good job.

I reach for a bag of potato chips, thinking of how the man in the ear had wanted the slice of life earlier. The corner of my mother's mouth starts to twitch as I crunch the chip.

"Did you send her over?" I ask the man in the ear. "Are we supposed to hash it out?"

No, he says. *We're working out today. Craig is waiting for us. He's the best trainer in L.A. We are going to do kettlebells and burpees and then get smoothies and talk about our goals.*

"I don't want to work out today," I tell him. "And I hate smoothies. Food should be chewed."

He laughs.

You should be a comedian, he says.

"Thanks," I say. It feels good to be understood.

My mother sits me down on the couch. She tells me she is here to stage an intervention. She thinks the show is bad for me. She says she hasn't met the producer, so she doesn't know if she can trust him.

"Why are the cameras hidden?" she asks. "What if the producer has bad intentions?"

"He doesn't," I say, confused.

She says she feels like she's being humiliated airing out her dirty laundry. She talked to my sister about her concerns and she agreed. I check my phone and see a message from Suzi. She says this is not the way to repair my relationship with my mother and I should keep my problems to myself. She says Thai people are supposed to smile. We don't talk about our problems in person and certainly not on television. We aren't supposed to have mother–daughter rifts.

"It's only thanks to him that we are spending time together," I tell her. "If he hadn't pushed me to drive down to Santa Ana, I wouldn't be talking to you."

"True," she says, arms crossed. "But that doesn't make it right. We need to get this guy out of here."

I plead with the man in the ear to tell my mother the show is good for us. He says I need to do the talking myself—I've never stood up to her. She doesn't respect my boundaries.

"You can't treat me like a kid anymore," I tell her. "All you do is criticize me, but I'm the one who kept the house going while you worked. I have a right to join a show if I want. This is my story and my life."

The words make her flinch. She looks guilty. I expect her to get defensive.

"I'm sorry," she finally says. This is the first time she has ever apologized to me. I'm so surprised I don't know what to say. "You gave up your childhood to watch Suzi," she continues. "It's the last thing I wanted for you. I didn't get a childhood either."

It makes me uncomfortable to see her sad.

"I'm sorry," I say.

My mother stands up suddenly and says she's tired. She seems off-balance as she gets into her car. There might be tears on her face. I've never seen her cry before, so I'm not sure what is happening to her eyes. Maybe it is better when she smiles.

"I messed up," I say to the man in the ear. "She's upset now."

He assures me I did the right thing by trying to start the conversation.

Give her some time, he says. *She'll understand.*

* * *

A FEW WEEKS LATER, my mother invites me over to her house for dinner. I feel grateful she isn't mad at me anymore. She doesn't mention the show. We have a nice, boring meal together. The kind I've craved my whole life. Drama-free.

"We don't have to talk about anything," I say.

"You were right," she says. "I should treat you like an adult."

"Really?" I ask, relieved.

She nods.

"You helped me with Suzi."

She's cooked my favorite dishes. Curry and bamboo shoots. Black sticky rice with coconut milk. I imagine a life in which we have dinner together every weekend. Did we have to be estranged? I feel like I made a mistake.

Afterward, the man in the ear says he has what he needs from me. We've wrapped up the arc with my mother. Next season we will get into my dating life and see if I can't grieve Nola more fully. Maybe then I'll let someone in. He tells me to have a good summer.

Stay out of trouble without me.

"That's it?" I ask. "You're leaving?"

I'll be back soon, he says.

"Did I do something wrong?" I ask. "Was the scene not good enough?"

"It was good," he says. "But now you're on better terms, so you don't need me. I'll be back when there's a conflict."

"Wait, don't go yet!" I shout, but there is only silence. "I miss you," I say. I leave the earpiece in, hoping he will come back. I already feel lonely again.

Later that day, as I work through my deliveries, I narrate where I'm going. "I'm headed to the Chop Stop to pick up three salads and a lemonade," I say, finding it soothing to speak into the ether, a rhythm I've gotten used to. "Customer didn't tip much, but I try to do my job well regardless. I take pride in that."

Then, as I'm parking, I hear a familiar voice in my ear, but it isn't the man. It's my mother.

What happened to the gym? she asks.

"How did you get in my ear?" I ask, startled.

You never took the earpiece out. Anyway, I bought you some new clothes. You're dressing more and more like a boy. You'll never get married looking like that, you know.

"I don't want to get married," I tell her. Which is only partially true. But my impulse is to argue.

My stomach tightens as I realize we've slid back into the same dynamic. The apology wasn't a real ending. The story is still going, even if the cameras are gone.

"Get out of my ear," I tell her. "I have to keep the line free. The producer might need something from me."

You don't need the show, she says. *You should move on.*

My mother doesn't leave. For weeks she stays there, nagging me. I consider removing the earpiece, but then I would lose my connection to the producer, and I don't want to do that.

A FEW MONTHS LATER, I get an invitation for the premiere. It's printed on the thickest piece of paper that has ever been inside my mailbox.

I buy a sequined dress from Macy's that matches my

shape closely enough. I book an appointment at a salon and get a mullet cut. I eat fruits and vegetables so my nails turn pink again. I'm surprised when this works. Through the earpiece, my mother tells me she thinks there will be eligible men at the premiere. I tell her to shut up and let me enjoy the night the way I want to enjoy it.

No one notices me as I exit the rideshare in front of the theater. There are beautiful women milling about. They are being photographed on the red carpet. I have no idea who they are and why they are the ones being photographed when the show is about me, but I am grateful there are people around to take the pressure off.

I bypass the red carpet and find a seat in the back row of the theater. The lights dim. The audience quiets in anticipation. I see my life cast on the screen: There I am in the prop house, my mother yelling at me. I scream at her about her boyfriends. She screams that I was supposed to be better than her and I have squandered the opportunity to have a real career. I ask her why she would have other expectations. "I am you," I tell her. "I never wanted to be like you," I say. "But that is what happened." My words shake her. At the end, she comes over to my house and apologizes for how she has treated me, her firstborn daughter. I tell her I forgive her. She hugs me.

I have no idea how they got this footage. I don't remember the apology scene happening quite this way, which irks me. There's nothing to show that the progress was undone soon after the apology. The screening ends with applause. There is a Q&A after. This is when I finally see the man in the ear. I can tell it's him by his voice. He wears a blue suit, blue shoes, and an argyle tie. He is a tiny man. For some reason, I pictured him large. I have so many questions for him, I don't know where to start. I wait until the end to raise my hand. The man is surprised to see me.

"D?" he asks. "You look so different—I didn't recognize you."

"Thank you," I say.

"I was hoping you would come," he says. "What did you think of our show?"

"It was pretty good," I tell him, even though the last scene made me feel uneasy.

He wipes his brow with his pink polka-dotted pocket square, which is folded into a triangular shape. I get hung up on the shape of the square—how can a pocket square be a triangle? Who would do such a thing to a square? I start to think of this as a bit I could do in a stand-up show. I am fixated on details that don't matter as a method of avoiding my discomfort. Once again I have found myself in a situation where I should speak up for myself.

This is my moment to ask what happened to my story. This is my chance to tell him that he fabricated a conversation that didn't exist. I could reclaim my narrative, but instead I blurt out a different question, one that I realize has been bothering me awhile.

"What was the show about when it was about Sven?" I ask. "What were the themes?"

"Why does it matter?" he asks.

"I want to know if I am more interesting than him," I say. It feels odd that I have no idea who Sven is, even after starring on a show named after him.

He laughs nervously, then walks out of the room. My mother has always said I don't understand how to be social with people. Maybe she's right.

I go home and have a drink by myself. Then I have another. The gaffe fades away and I like myself again. All it takes is a drink or two. I pick up the phone and text Nikita a photo I found on the internet of someone in her underwear.

You shouldn't be drinking, my mother says. *You want to be like Grandma now?*

"Oh, is that what this feeling is?" I ask. "How do you know I'm drinking? Are there cameras in here too?"

She doesn't answer.

As I finish off my third glass of whiskey, I feel my grandmother flickering inside me, but I'm disappointed to hear my mother has compared us. Drinking makes me feel good. Alcohol is my only path to an authentic, outgoing self. There is no self that is worth salvaging without it.

I peel off the dress and change back into my gym shorts. I turn on the TV. My show is on again—a midnight repeat. The guide shows it running all night. I can't listen to the sound of my own voice, so I keep it on mute. If only Nola were here with me. I imagine us hate-watching it over potstickers and cheese puffs. That's how we watched *Felicity.* She relentlessly mocked it. I never told her I secretly loved that show—that I loved watching any shows about friends.

You can't spend the rest of your life mourning a dead girl, my mother says from my ear. *You need to move on. Let someone else in.*

She keeps talking, but I tune her out. It's one thing to be told what to wear or eat but another to be told how to think about the person I love. I don't want to let anyone else in. I want to live in the reality in which I told Nola my feelings and she didn't go for a run on the day of her accident. The life I could have had if only two moments were different. I hear my mother clearing her throat, as she often does before she talks. But she doesn't say anything. She doesn't have to speak for me to hear the criticism.

The next morning, I go back to the park where I first heard about Sven. I take the earpiece out and leave it on the bench where I found it. Silence is a soundtrack I can live with.

MUSCLE TO MUSCLE, TOE TO TOE

They were both 35–44 / progressive / quirky / chronically ill / partially unwhite / travel-intrigued dreamers / likely to click on videos of funiculars in the Swiss Alps—yet it took them nearly ten years to cross paths.

They bumped into each other at the dance store. M had been alone since college and no longer expected to meet someone. She wasn't going to be one of those people who settled down just because she was getting older. She wasn't scared of aging. Studies showed that women were happier alone. It was men who needed a partner to take care of them, men who were diminished living alone. And maybe there was a part of her that was insecure about her illness, but she tried not to think about her disease when she was in remission.

She was not looking for love when she saw X. He was tall and angular, with long arms and soft dreadlocks. He wore a plain black T-shirt with a hole in the bottom, near the hem. He had picked out the same model of tap shoe as she had, but in white. He was almost at the register with the box tucked under his arm when he noticed her smiling at him. He started talking first, rambling on about a Blip he'd seen earlier, some kids dancing to "Breezeblocks."

"The joy on their faces," X said. "I was in a troupe when I was a kid. I was never happier than when I danced."

M had seen the same Blip herself this morning, on her phone, over cinnamon toast, alone in her apartment, and had thought, why not dance again? She had been in a tap troupe herself as a kid.

"I rarely use my body like that anymore," M said. "I set it down in a chair and leave it there while I work at my computer all day. I spend my whole life on the computer or the phone."

"It's time to move again," X said, nodding.

"Are you me?" M said. "What are the odds we were both in dance troupes as kids and we saw the same video today?"

X flashed her a silly grin.

"Kismet," he said.

They left the store together and kept walking for a while. They didn't have to speak much to feel like they were getting to know each other. And then he slipped his real hand into her real fingers, his skin on her skin.

LATER THAT WEEK, M went over to X's apartment. As she walked in, she saw that the shoes weren't their only shared purchase. By the entrance hung her chevron coat. She spotted her hovering-moon lamp on the hallway table. The moon levitated above its base and provided enough light for a small room. M had bought it from an artist online, maybe on Kickstarter, though she couldn't remember.

As she walked deeper into X's apartment she saw her boxing sneakers, her blue velvet couch, her white tile kitchen, her claw-foot tub, her calathea plant that got sad at night. X told her the calathea was the only plant he'd ever owned that had feelings. He claimed it was a Dorian Gray situation—he rarely had feelings of his own and had probably transferred his melancholy over to the plant. She couldn't tell if he was joking. She asked him why he didn't have feelings. He shrugged. Something about a hard childhood. M could see she wouldn't get more out of him, but she liked a person who didn't talk much. Silence was her default choice. His silence made her want to kiss him.

Later that night, she took him to her house down the hill to show him her hovering-moon lamp, her boxing sneakers, and her melancholy plant. It was cold out. She could barely feel her fingers as she turned the key in the front door.

"Just a second," she said. "I need to tidy up."

She left him at the doorway. She could hear him tapping in the hall. She heard him do wings and a time step. The living room was a mess. No one ever came home with her. She moved her cane into the closet. There was no need for him to know that she sometimes struggled with balance, that she could lose her hearing, her sight. Her disease hadn't flared up in a few years. As X tapped through the time steps in the hallway, she answered with a few toe-stand turns of her own.

* * *

A FEW MONTHS LATER, they were married in a small courthouse ceremony attended only by their siblings. There was no budget for a wedding. The money went toward an elaborate multi-stop honeymoon. It was easy to plan the trip—M and X had bookmarked the same Blips before they'd met.

They began the trip in Italy, where they swam the impossibly turquoise waters of Sardinia and drank limoncellos on balconies of pastel Positano hotels. From there, they chartered a boat to Capri, where M dove into the water and swallowed what felt like the entire sea. She liked the moment the salt water passed through her nose, even though her crevices burned. For a few seconds, she felt like the earth. It was an experience that caught her by surprise, one that couldn't be captured in videos. X tap-danced on the balcony. The tourists gathered to watch from below. She marveled at how just last year, they were both sitting alone in their living rooms, clicking on Blips, wishing they were somewhere else. But now they were inside the videos. They were making new ones.

A second leg took them to Machu Picchu and the Rainbow Mountains of Peru. The last leg brought them to the Galápagos for a cruise. They spent their days snorkeling off the boat. The water was surprisingly cold, thanks to the Humboldt Current from Antarctica, another sensation that couldn't have been caught in a video. It felt good to shiver in these equatorial waters. The sun burned her skin, but the water was cold. M felt overwhelmed by the bright candy hues, the most breathtaking vistas on earth. She'd never been happier than when she swam with penguins off Bartolomé Island.

X jumped off the boat and screamed like a kid. His asthma had become so debilitating that he never imagined he could hike up a hill, yet here he was, snorkeling unprotected waters in the Pacific.

"You make me healthy," he told M. "I used to be so depressed I couldn't breathe."

"We make each other healthy," M said.

BACK HOME, THE YOUNG couple successfully transitioned to domestic bliss: brunches with farmers-market fruits, homemade pickles, fresh-baked loaves of sourdough bread—a life made popular on Blips. On their one-year anniversary, M gifted X an apron embroidered with his name. She bought it in cherry red so it would pop against the white kitchen backsplash in their photographs. X felt proud in the apron. He felt like a grown-up husband.

Their marriage was idyllic until X got lunch with his friend S, who worked as an executive at a social-media startup and was in town on business.

"I'd never felt like this about someone I'd just met," X said, filling his friend in.

"What's she like?" asked S, tilting his head. Though they were roommates in college, it had been a couple of years since they'd caught up with each other.

"Every day is the best day of my life," X explained. "I don't understand people who marry the wrong person and feel miserable. It's not so difficult to do it right, is it?"

S nodded. He finished off his pineapple basil slushy and

tucked away the hand-painted jar in his bag for later. Businesses had been stepping up their game in the years since social media started featuring photographs instead of words. The world was slowly becoming more beautiful thanks to tech. Every outing was a carefully curated visual experience, meant to be shared not just with friends but with strangers.

"When I bumped into M, I felt like I'd known her my whole life," X went on. "It was uncanny. I must be a very lucky person. She has the same hovering-moon lamp as me. I don't remember where I got that thing. Some random Kickstarter, I think . . . In fact, we have a lot of the same stuff. Poetic, isn't it?"

"Are you both on Blips?" S asked.

X nodded.

"And how much of the same stuff have you bought?" S asked.

"I'd say at least a dozen unique objects in common," X said. "And we both used to tap-dance when we were kids. It's funny how similar we are."

"I'd venture to guess you both saw an ad for the same lamp," S said. "You must be in the same marketing niche. There's no other way to explain the coincidence—it's the algorithm."

M frowned. He trusted that S was familiar with the business end of Blips; he'd worked there for a stint before joining his current start-up. But M didn't want to believe that an algorithm, and not kismet, could be responsible for their relationship. He stood up quickly and searched for the exit. The people at the next table stopped their conversation, looking over at them. He felt sick.

"Don't get so upset," S said. "The algorithm ensures

you'll continue to have common interests as you age. No fighting about where to go on vacay. You have similar spending priorities—it's good for marriage longevity."

But the news didn't sit well with X. He went for a walk around the neighborhood to sort out his thoughts. M hadn't lied to him. She was the same good person who loved him, but he felt their love was cheapened by the algorithm. Who knew what kind of people they would be if they hadn't been influenced? Perhaps they would have little in common. It wasn't just the ads they had clicked. They had probably spent years reading the same curated articles too. The algorithm had molded them into the same person. There could be hundreds of other Ms out there, for all he knew.

X had always felt like he was too damaged for a real relationship. He had struggled with depression since high school. How could a person love him when he hated himself? He knew he carried baggage from childhood, but when he met M, he was impressed she had managed to break through his aloof façade. He thought it must have been a sign there was something real between them. But maybe he had been waiting for the other shoe to drop since they'd met.

When he got home, M was cutting flowers in the kitchen. Her back looked beautiful in a tank top. He wondered if he could look past the algorithm, but he couldn't forget. His inner critic was more powerful than any algorithm. It influenced him to make the wrong choices—but this was an insight that would come to him years later.

It took him another week to work up the courage to tell her. She could sense something was wrong. He had pulled back and had started to come home late, after she was asleep. He wanted to be sure he was making the right decision.

One morning, over breakfast, he delivered the breakup message robotically, like he was ordering from a menu. Their relationship was merely a byproduct of advertising—no different from a plastic grocery bag that came out of the process of oil refinement. He said the mystery was gone. Life was about magic moments that were unexplainable. He was going to unplug and see if he could recapture a life that wasn't guided by an algorithm. He didn't look at M as he spoke. After he left, he deleted his socials and never contacted her again.

THE STRESS OF THE breakup triggered M into the worst flare of her life. She lost her vision first, then her balance, then her hearing. She took it easy for a few days, but the disease took hold. Her family lived too far away to help, but there were apps that would deliver food, shuttle her to appointments, and provide her with a home nurse. Her doctors worked out new combinations of medications. It was trial and error, they said. Throw pasta at a wall and see what sticks. Sometimes her sight returned, sometimes her balance, sometimes her hearing, but each time, progress faded just as quickly as it came.

The medication made her itchy. This feeling was intolerable when she couldn't see and her other senses were heightened. Her limbs twitched. Every so often, a neighbor stopped by, and she was grateful for the help.

* * *

IT TOOK TWO YEARS for M to feel better. Her senses returned and she could walk. She was even able to tap-dance. The muscle memory was intact. She no longer felt exhausted, which was good because it took strength to claw her way back. After two years in isolation, she no longer wished to be alone. She went out to coffee shops and shows. Her real life would begin now. The sick years would fade away, unimportant in her story.

She felt good as she walked through the gloomy streets, even as tiny raindrops clung to her skin. The air was so clean and crisp she could eat it like an apple. She found it thrilling to experience the world with every sense.

She wasn't mad at the existence of the algorithm. It gave her a reason to be optimistic. There could be another X. But then as she got to thinking, she decided she didn't want another X. She had watched the wrong Blips and had attracted someone who was fragile and depressed. This time she would attract someone better. She had interests that she didn't share with X—like the environment. Her ideal partner would care deeply about the earth. He would be a calm person. Unflappable even. He would be smarter and stronger than her. She searched for yoga classes, meditation podcasts, and mindfulness coaches so the algorithm would make her attractive to this person.

It wasn't long before her feed started to shift. She was no longer shown beautiful travel videos. Instead, she saw images of disaster. People dying of hunger, drying rivers filled with bones, cities on fire, countries under water. It was difficult for her to keep from feeling anxious watching these kinds of videos. In between such articles were ads for sustainable yoga mats that would melt into the earth, leaving behind no trace, for a guilt-free meditation. She bought one of these mats even though it was expensive.

SHE SAW V FOR the first time at a coffee shop. He had long black hair with silver streaks. His face was handsome, though his skin was slightly cracked. There was a disappearing yoga mat strapped to his back. She had never encountered another person who had bought one before. A sign. He was reading the news made out of paper. She thought it was charming. She once knew a man who paid for all purchases in two-dollar bills he got from the bank every Monday. She had probably seen a newspaper as often as she had seen a two-dollar bill.

She couldn't help but stare. Someone should do a Blip crinkling newspapers, she thought—though they would never be able to capture the way that these papers smelled. She watched him turn the pages for a bit. She wanted to crunch the paper in her hands, squeeze it into balls in her fists. Real-life ASMR. Good thing she put on a dress today. She wanted badly to impress him. Then he glanced up at her. She could tell he thought she was cute.

"Where do you find a newspaper?" she asked.

"There's a store in Georgetown that sells them," he says.

He invited her to sit with him.

"You can touch it if you want," he said, handing her the newspaper.

As she leafed through it, he told her that he worked as a cardiologist. He had just come back from a month spent volunteering with tribes in the Amazon and was still decompressing from the experience. M was impressed.

"Do you volunteer too?" he asked.

"I'm looking into some opportunities," she said, even though she wasn't.

"I know some women's health clinics that could use some help," he said. "I could put you in touch. You must be passionate about reproductive rights."

She nodded. She *was* passionate, though she had done nothing to support the cause. Already, V was pushing her to be better.

M wasn't usually so forward, but she asked V to walk her home. They stopped for oat milk ice cream over by the hospital. Better for the environment than regular ice cream, he said. I know, she told him. She'd read the same article. He said he was sailing to Victoria this weekend but suggested they get drinks when he was back. M was sure she had found the person she was looking for—someone better than her. Her plan had worked. She wouldn't tell him about her illness or her divorce. She wouldn't tell him she spent years on her phone, watching travel Blips. She would hide the worst parts of her. This was her chance to build a life with someone who cured people.

In preparation for their date, M read up on sailing and watched YouTube tutorials. Now that she knew the algorithm was listening, she made spreadsheets documenting all of V's interests. She needed to see the right ads and read the same articles so she could be shaped into his perfect match. Every time he sent her a text, she searched for relevant terms so she could become a V expert.

* * *

WHEN V RETURNED FROM his trip, they got drinks at the café near the university. M had learned so much about sailing that she was able to pass as a boat nut. He suggested they go out together the next weekend with good weather, but M wasn't confident she could keep up the ruse on a real boat, so she made up an excuse as their sailing date approached. When V mentioned a subject M couldn't understand, she would make a joke and deflect, then return to it later, once she'd had a chance to research. She studied the rules of rugby. She taught herself Go. The first few weeks of dating it was hard to keep up, but after a while she could see her work paying off.

Their relationship went smoothly for a few months, until V revealed that he was looking to settle down with a woman who wanted kids. He was forty-five and feeling his age.

"No one will discover me once I turn forty-six," V said. "Women set forty-five as a limit on the apps, so it will be like I don't exist. If I don't get married this year, it will be too late. What do you think? I like you a lot, but do you want kids?"

M nodded enthusiastically. She didn't want kids, but she could work at it, learn to want them. She had come so far already by shaping herself as V's ideal girlfriend. Why let a difference of opinion break up this relationship?

"Our kids will be beautiful," he said, stroking her chin. "And smart too. We'll make the world a better place one baby at a time."

"How many babies will there be?" she asked, trying not to sound alarmed.

"I wanted nine," V said. "But I'd settle for three. One of each. Small, medium, and large."

M nodded.

"I'd love to have a little feminist," he said.

V wanted to start preparing now, given his advanced age. He told her it was important to eat healthy and pulled a chocolate bar out of her mouth. He said her pre-pregnancy snacks could affect their kids.

"No junk food," he said. "And let's take it easy on the GMOs. No pesticides either. You may think vegetables are healthy, but we need to know where our food is sourced. We could end up with sick children."

"Sick children?" she asked.

"You haven't read about the soil?" he said.

She shook her head, concerned there was a blind spot in her news algorithm. They were supposed to be in sync—buying the same things, clicking the same links.

"Did you read about the soil in the paper news?" M asked, confused.

"I don't actually read newspapers," V said. "I take them to coffee shops for fun, to pick up chicks. They like that kind of thing. But now I don't need newspapers. I have my chick."

He pinched her cheek, maybe because it sounded like chick. Later, she searched for news about the soil and found it was contaminated with heavy metals from industrial waste and the long-term use of phosphate fertilizers. Rice was one of the most affected crops, full of arsenic. She had grown up on rice, but it wasn't fit for human consumption. Even worse, the big fruit farms were using chemicals to make brighter, more perfect fruits. Fruits worth posting in Blips.

V made her juices from his homegrown tomatoes. He subscribed to a box of ugly vegetables—the ones deemed safest for small children. Vegetables that looked like Qs and

Ws. She ate one with each meal, but she missed round apples, pear-shaped pears.

"Are you sure you want to bring a child into this world?" she asked one day over dinner. "It seems like a bad place. The toxins, you know?"

"We'll make it better," he said.

M still didn't want to be a mother, but she didn't want to be alone either. V made her feel safe. She had stupidly been eating poisoned vegetables just because they were beautiful. She needed V—he was smarter than her. Maybe one day he would stop wanting a small, medium, and large. Maybe her own feelings toward motherhood would change if she clicked on more links.

But M got pregnant sooner than she expected. Her hands shook as she picked up the test. She had been sensing her body was no longer her own, but the double lines confirmed it.

"We're pregnant!" V shouted.

He picked her up and swung her by the ankles like a dancer. He tossed her onto the couch like a stuffed animal. He threw her into the bed and made love to her, but love was the last thing she wanted to make. He stopped to dab the tears in her eyes. He thought they were tears of joy.

She spent the next several months trying to talk herself into the transition, but as she grew more pregnant, she worried she had made a terrible mistake. She should have waited for another X instead of trying to outsmart the algorithm. But Little M was cooking, moving, already a person. With her tiny fetal hands, she had pushed M's belly and shoved the kitchen table away from them.

* * *

THE BABY CAME EARLY, with complications. The doctors had to make several large incisions to get it out. The nurses set Little M on her chest, bloody, and M tried to imagine the happiness she could feel. A baby. Hers. V was on the other side of the curtain for a moment, across the operation theater.

"Why do they call it a theater?" she asked. No one answered.

Little M was only five pounds. M apologized to her as a first order of business.

"I'm sorry you're small," she said. "It's my fault. Something I ate. I didn't always research the metal content. Sometimes I got lazy and ate lead."

"Hush," V said, from the other side of the curtain. "Pull yourself together. You're a mother now. You need to put on your best front."

"I'm just a person with a hole in my belly," she said. "I'm not a mother yet. I'll let you know when I start, okay? Maybe tomorrow? I want one last day before I become someone else."

V seemed confused by M's request, but he didn't object. It took half an hour to stitch her body back together. They told her it wasn't a normal cesarean—that they had to cut more than usual. She didn't know much about what was happening on the other side of the curtain. Her lower half was numb. She was in the middle of a magic trick with dummy legs, except they were her legs, her magic trick. *Ta-da, a baby came out of you,* she whispered. *Ta-da, never thought you would be a mother, did you?*

Before they finished stitching her up, they snatched the

baby off her chest. Little M had to go to the NICU, they said. She was too small and not good at breathing.

"You can visit later," the doctor said. "When you're whole."

"When will I be whole?" she asked.

She was still numb and had no idea what was happening in the half of her that was behind the curtain. This felt worse than when she lost her balance. Would the lower half come back, or would she just be a stump in bed, just an upper half? She had many fears to work through, but this story was no longer about her. Everyone wanted to talk about the baby. This was fair. The baby had some serious problems right now, more serious than hers. Little M needed help to make it out of this hospital alive.

M WAS DISCHARGED AFTER a few days, but the baby remained in the NICU. After some touch-and-go weeks, the baby learned how to eat. They were able to take her home and start their new life. M spent most of the day with the baby at her breast, her own body stiff and foreign.

Tomorrow I will feel like a mother, she told herself. *I will wake up to a new day and it will be the real beginning.*

But there were no such things as separate days now, nothing to help demarcate this new chapter. As soon as the baby stopped eating, she needed to eat again. If she was full, it was time for a diaper change. V didn't change any diapers, though he tried to be helpful in his own way. He made ugly-food smoothies, but soon he went back to work. Patients would die without him, he said. M couldn't protest. She didn't want anyone to die on her account, even if she thought she might die herself. Somehow she managed, though she missed having him around to bring her food at night.

When Little M was eight weeks, V went on a sailing trip with his buddies. He left them for three long days. It was terrifying to be alone. She could feel her disease flaring up, first in her bones and in her limbs. Then her vision went out. It was tough at first, but she found she could still manage to give Little M her milk.

When V came home, he found M on the floor, patting the rug to look for the diaper cream.

"What are you doing down there?" he asked.

"I dropped something," she said.

She asked about his trip as a distraction, but he had already picked up on her blindness. She had no choice but to explain.

"You're sick?" he asked. "Why didn't you tell me?"

"I'm sorry," she said. "It hardly ever happens. I'll be fine. I just need my medicine."

V was silent. She couldn't see his face, so she had no idea what he was thinking.

"Are you mad?" she asked.

She pushed herself to her feet and walked over to the spot where she had last heard V's voice, but he wasn't there anymore. She turned toward what she thought was the door, but then V's voice came booming over from the other side of the room.

"You lied to me," he said. "You never said you were sick."

"You think I wanted this life?" she asked, her voice shaking.

"What do you mean?" he asked.

M debated whether she wanted to get into it. The baby cried from the Boppy in one corner of the room. V coughed in another.

"You were the one who wanted children," she said. "But you left me alone to do all the work. I needed help." Perhaps there had been warning signs that V was old-fashioned, but she suddenly felt tricked into being his wife. He wasn't the only one who had been lied to.

"So what now?" V asked.

"I don't know," M said.

V said he was taking Little M to his mother's house. He needed some time to think. The door shut behind them before she could protest.

The next day, he came home with the baby and his mother, G, in tow. He said he was sorry that he didn't realize how much of a toll the childcare would take but his mother could help. G begged M to recognize how much pressure V was under at the hospital. He worked long hours and had little time left over for himself. His mother took over feeding and diapering. M felt a burden lift. She was able to rest and focus on her recovery. After a few weeks, she got better.

When she could see again, she examined V's face carefully. She'd crafted herself to suit him. She'd thought he was better than her. But he wasn't. He was flawed too.

At least now that his mother was around, V seemed less stressed. As time went on, he learned how to support M. He drove her to medical appointments. He changed some diapers. Then, at six months, Little M moved out of their room and into a crib down the hallway. M slept through the night for the first time, and she thought just maybe she could do this.

* * *

SHE SEARCHED FOR X online sometimes. She wondered if he had found peace, another M—if his life had ended up better than hers. But she couldn't find anything about him. He had stayed true to his word, living off the grid, away from the algorithm. She hoped that his heart had guided him well. Maybe he was tap-dancing around the world by himself.

Sometimes she looked at the old Blips that had led her to him—the tap-dancing kids, the Blips that had inspired their honeymoon. The videos stirred nothing in her now. She could barely remember what it felt like to swim with the penguins in the Galápagos, though only five years had passed since that moment. It was a good thing the equatorial water was cold or maybe she wouldn't be able to recall the memory as an experience distinct from the video. But in time, as her daughter grew older and M grew used to being a mother, she began to think of the water as warm.

ANOTHER TOAD IN THE FEELY BOX

Bird sleeps in and is late for work. It's eleven A.M., an unacceptable time to make an appearance. She is the assistant program manager at a Portland children's museum. Her boss, Mr. P, will know she is lying if she claims she is sick. He is always looking for a reason to put her down. He is generally a difficult person.

When Mr. P is unstimulated, he is known to fill the "feely boxes" with crickets, toads, or chicken feet. Every day on her way to her desk, she checks the sensory-box exhibit to make sure that the children are not exposed to anything upsetting.

Bird has felt unhappy at her job for a few years. She hasn't quit because it is her duty to ensure the grope boxes do not disturb the children. But she thinks today is the day. She cannot stomach the look Mr. P will give her when she arrives late. She worries he is close to making a move. Last week he suggested she date an older man. Someone experienced. He tells her smart girls get married in their twenties. He says she is lucky to be brimming with sexual energy, despite her age. He says she might still be able to get married, but only if she acts soon. Mr. P is a bachelor at fifty-one. He dresses in cardigans and wears shiny leather shoes, like he belongs in a fancier place—perhaps at a university—but he has chosen to make his life at a children's museum.

She doesn't have enough money saved up for college yet, but she has enough for a buffer while she looks for a new job. No need to subject herself to more harassment by going in late. Mr. P will tell her she is acting like a teenager. He will ask her what she was up to late last night. If the fun was worth it. He will follow this up with a compliment about her blouse.

She texts him her resignation. He responds with a flurry of messages. He asks if she's joking. He tells her he needs her. He offers her a raise. He asks if they are still friends. He sends a photo of his outfit and asks how he looks. She deletes the rest of his texts without reading them.

It feels good to be free of Mr. P. Now that she's quit, she realizes how much she'd internalized his criticism. She is hopeful she can finally take the next step. But over the next few days, she finds it difficult to take initiative. She is overwhelmed. Leaving her job has been disruptive to her life rhythms. She no longer has a reason to get dressed. She makes no progress on her portfolio. She feels depressed.

Finally, she forces herself to leave the house. She finds a

guy at a jazz club who looks all right. He is wearing a soft shirt she likes. He comes into her apartment for a drink, but before he kisses her, he asks to turn off the smart vacuum. The vacuum was a gift from Mr. P. It is the nicest thing she owns. It makes her feel rich. She usually leaves it running.

He says he feels strange having sex in front of the vacuum. He's against high-tech objects that don't need to be high tech. He brags that he uses only a smartphone. She tells him she worries more about her smartphone than any other object. It's impossible to be unreachable when she wants to disconnect. But she sees nothing wrong with a clean house, so she leaves the vacuum running.

VEE IS PAID THIRTY-SIX cents an hour to review the footage that comes in through the robot vacuum cleaner. It is not much money, but she is unable to walk well after a motorbike racing accident damaged her right leg. She doesn't have much feeling in it, though she is in physical therapy and hopes to regain more sensation. She is grateful to have any job while she learns to walk without a cane again. She has moved back in with her mother temporarily. She is still young. There is plenty of time ahead of her.

She was just starting her life when the accident happened. She had secured a sponsorship deal with an American sports-apparel company, but that money went toward her medical expenses. After the injury, she was relieved to find work in video transcription. She is assigned videos and uploads the notes to a server each night. She has no idea what happens to the notes after that. She doesn't ask questions.

Vee's last job involved watching a man cheat on his wife

while the vacuum worked the floor beneath him. She found it difficult to watch him interact with his wife after seeing how he behaved while she was at her yoga class. She was relieved to switch to the new girl, who sketches in her free time. The girl is uncomplicated and easy to watch. There is a pleasing rhythm to her movements. At first, Vee logged the girl's activities after she came home from work. Even as the girl ate dinner, there was often a look on her face that was hard to convey in note form, like she was always thinking through something important. One night she painted herself in the nude using her reflection in the mirror.

A few weeks later, the girl suddenly stops leaving the house. She sleeps whether it is day or night. Some days she eats too much and other days she eats nothing at all. She sleeps on a pink donut. The donut remains on her shoulder for six days until she takes a shower.

Vee worries the girl is depressed. She recognizes the signs. She has been depressed herself since her accident. The hunger for adrenaline still tugs at her. She wants to win. She has lost her sense of self. She hates living at home while she is recovering. She manages her pain by distracting herself with work. Even mindless typing helps. She feels a connection to this girl, who is probably only a few years older than her, so she starts to write fake notes to cover for her. She doesn't know how the information is being used, and her instinct is to protect her, so she makes up a day in which the girl goes to work and comes home late. She thinks it is important to portray the girl as a productive person.

* * *

BIRD STOPS TAKING HER anti-anxiety medication. It feels like too much effort to get herself a glass of water. A few days later, she has a full-blown panic attack and curls up in her closet. She is scared to be alone. She doesn't know when to eat or how to separate the parts of the day. Her thoughts run together. Every hour feels the same.

Her mental state slips away from her before she recognizes the signs. It usually takes her several days to understand what is happening, even though she's had other bouts with depression.

She was thirteen when she learned her parents were in a fake marriage. Her father had started another family in Phoenix, with a daughter and son a few years younger than her. He saw them on his frequent "business trips." Her brother, Royce, had discovered the news while going through some emails. He brought the evidence to their mother, only to find out she already knew. She said she didn't want to destroy the family. That some things were better kept secret. Bird felt terrible letting her father get away with the affair, as if she was complicit in destroying the family. That's when her panic attacks started. She would feel like she was floating away from herself. Sometimes, she was so lonely that she fantasized about meeting the ghost siblings, but she was not allowed to acknowledge their existence. Her mother still requires they pretend the other family doesn't exist.

Royce can help her snap out of her current funk. He is a reliable person. She decides she will visit him. It is difficult to pack for a trip of indeterminate length, so she doesn't. She leaves with only her purse, as if she's going out to the store. The trip down to San Francisco is ten hours. She drives it in one go, stopping only for gas and bathroom breaks. She leaves her car at the end of his driveway, blocking in his. There is no parking in his part of the Mission.

Royce welcomes her in even though he is surprised to see her.

"I needed to get away for a bit," she tells him.

"Stay as long as you want," he says. "But get your car out of my driveway first."

"Later," she says. She is too tired to look for parking.

She follows him in. She feels better as soon as she enters the large house. It is well-decorated, like a Victorian film set. He says his kids are at school and his wife is at a conference she has extended into a vacation, which is a relief. Bird finds it harder to talk to Royce candidly when Jessica is around. She worries her sister-in-law doesn't enjoy her presence.

Royce is the smarter sibling, though by his own standards he is not smart enough. Several years ago he founded Hearts, a social-media app that focuses on maintaining privacy. He designed it to allow users to share content within a small circle of real-life friends. The interface looks like a piece of art. Royce was a better painter than her. He could have gone to art school, but he was also good at coding and wanted to make the world a better place.

Hearts gained a cult following but eventually ran out of funding. Royce was forced to sell to a tech giant, which meant he was paid a nice sum to become a regular employee. He bought this house with his money, but he is bitter. He would rather have the app. The acquiring company is slowly dismantling the product by cramming multiple ads in between every post—one last money grab before they shut it down and sell the data abroad. Her brother has been sad this year for the first time since she can remember. When he was designing the app, it never occurred to him he would lose control of it.

He tells her he doesn't know why some companies are allowed to be unprofitable while others are not. He says that most apps have no path to making money, yet many of them continue to be propped up by venture-capital funds. Bird doesn't know enough about start-up finance to follow every nuance of the conversation, but what Royce says makes sense.

"Maybe they'll change their mind," she tells him.

"We're probably the last two people using it," he says.

"Jessica's not on it?" Bird asks.

"She's on it," he says cryptically. He offers her green-tea pastries he purchased from the bakery across the street. "They make a fine last meal. I have them special-ordered every day just in case."

She laughs, but his joke disturbs her. She worries about his mental state. He has put his entire adult life into building the app, and it doesn't have much time left. She hopes he will be able to move on.

Later, his children come home from school. They are nine and six. A girl, Lee, and a boy, Tom. They fling themselves onto their father's limbs, and he runs around the room like an airplane. They collapse into a pile and tickle one another. Bird is impressed that her brother has been able to build a real family, despite the one they came from.

They eat takeout dinner at his large table. His mother-in-law joins them, though she doesn't participate in the conversation, because she speaks little English. Instead, she focuses on feeding the children, freeing Royce to catch up with Bird.

After dinner, the mother-in-law follows them around the house with a broom. Bird feels uncomfortable speaking freely in front of her, but Royce assures her she doesn't understand what they are saying. He tells her the mother-in-law's name, but Bird quickly forgets it. He tells her that she has moved in recently to help with the kids.

"Have you talked to Mom lately?" Royce asks.

Bird shakes her head. She tenses, waiting for bad news. Every time the phone rings, she prepares herself. Whenever her mother was in the bathroom too long, Bird used to pound on the door. She imagined her dead on the floor, but usually she was plucking out her grays. Now she imagines her mother is in the hospital, that Royce has been sparing her the truth. But Royce doesn't share bad news.

"She's taken up ballroom dancing," he tells her.

"Really?" she asks, laughing.

He nods. "You should ask her about it," he says. "She likes the cha-cha best."

"I need to see this," Bird says.

"Ask her to add you to the rehearsal-video album," he says.

"There's an album?" Bird asks. "Who else is on it?"

"Just me, I think," Royce says. "And Aunt Dang."

He shows her a video their mother recently uploaded. Their mother cuddles up to her instructor and uses a hip action that Bird is unfamiliar with. She feels disturbed seeing her mother grind on a young Russian man, even though the move is choreographed.

"I didn't know she could do that with her hips," Bird says.

"I didn't either," Royce says.

"Go, Mom," Bird says. "You're such a good son, commenting on her videos."

"You could comment," Royce says.

"She loves you more," Bird says. "She named you after the car she wanted. She named me after the most helpless thing in the yard."

Bird thinks if she had a better nickname, she wouldn't be so diminutive—too many Thai nicknames are diminutive. Maybe if her mother had stood up to her father, Bird wouldn't have stayed at her job working with Mr. P for so long. Bird wonders if she, too, will still be looking for ways to fill her time when she is her mother's age. Her life could become just as precarious if she isn't able to secure a new job. She needs to get out of this fog that she's in.

Royce lets her comment go without asking a follow-up question. He knows she's come here because she doesn't feel well, but they rarely speak directly about their problems. He helps in other ways. Like letting her stay in his house as long as she wants.

THE GIRL HAS BEEN gone for two days, though the vacuum continues to suck up dust. It is not normal for her to be gone for this long. Vee worries something bad has happened. She searches the news for a missing woman in Portland, but there are no reports that match her description. She rewinds through the footage, looking for clues. The girl had walked out the door without a suitcase. She was wearing pink sweats, a red sweater, and two different boots. Vee finds it unlikely she meant to go somewhere farther than a store.

When she fast-forwards to real time, she finds the vacuum stuck in a corner. It repeatedly slams into a wall. Normally when this happens, the girl sets the vacuum back on course, but there is no one here to reposition the vacuum. It causes Vee anxiety to watch the camera slam into the wall.

She reaches for her cane and pushes herself up. Normally on Sundays she forces herself to walk eight blocks to the meatball shop on Sukhumvit. It is a challenge, but she likes to get out of the house. Her mother urges her to stay home and rest, but Vee would rather be outside, feeling human. She spends too much time on the computer. She feels like an accessory to it. She figures if she tries hard enough, she will walk well again.

Down at the meatball shop, she runs into her sister, Nu—a large woman with short hair. They are friendly but not in touch often. Nu has moved across the city to start law school, and she doesn't have much free time. Vee misses the closeness they shared as kids. When her sister entered law school, Vee felt like she'd died. Since then, Nu has been distracted by her work. She came to visit Vee in the hospital once but couldn't take more time off from her studies. She seems shocked to see her now.

"You can walk this far?" Nu asks. "You should have told me you wanted meatballs. I could have brought them."

"Exercise is good for me," Vee tells her. She decides to lie. "I have a tour booked. Sponsors to please. I need to rehab my leg quickly or they'll drop me."

"That's good you didn't lose your sponsors after the accident," Nu says, surprised. "I thought for sure they'd be gone."

"It's like breaking a leg," Vee says. "Twelve more weeks and I should be back to normal."

"Mom really exaggerates, huh?" Nu asks. "She had me worried you were a cripple."

"That's ridiculous," Vee says. She doesn't want to hear how people talk about her. "What are you doing here?" she asks.

"I had to pick up some books," Nu says, gesturing toward the bookstore nearby. She pats Vee's back and tells her she has an extra room if she gets sick of living with their mom. Nu says she is rarely home. She spends most of her time studying at the library.

Vee takes her meatballs to a dusty bench by the bus stop and contemplates the offer. She would rather be in Nu's condo than at her mother's house, but then her sister would see how much she is struggling. Vee doesn't want her to know how difficult it is for her to do her daily chores. She wears loose shorts now because they are the easiest to put on. She doesn't feel attractive anymore. She can't exercise. All she can do is eat, listen, and type.

BIRD ENJOYS A BATH in her brother's deep soaking tub. She slathers herself with handcrafted soaps from the boutiques on Valencia. She stays in the bath for over an hour. Though Royce sees the house as a consolation prize, she feels like he should appreciate it more. It's pleasant here. Isn't the point of work to get rich? Is there a way to participate halfway in the system of capitalism? He is thriving inside, while she is living on the outside, barely able to scrape up the money to go to art school, which will fulfill her but lead to few job prospects. She thinks he has the dream life, even if he doesn't see it.

Once her brother goes to work and the children go to school, she is left alone with the mother-in-law, who silently sweeps the stairs.

"Beautiful day," Bird says.

The mother-in-law stares and doesn't say anything. Bird finds her gaze uncomfortable, so she hurries out of the house. She spends the rest of the day roller-skating in Golden Gate Park. She hasn't skated in years, but it comes back quickly to her. Deep inside her core, something works to keep her steady.

After a week at her brother's San Francisco house, Bird starts to feel better. Every day spent in her brother's home feels like a vacation. She eats ten-dollar oranges and applies creams to her feet. Her ankles are sore from roller-skating each day, but it is a good kind of sore, a feeling of exertion she hasn't had in a while. The creams soften the calluses.

Later, at dinner, as the mother-in-law sweeps the crumbs from under the table, Bird asks her brother why he doesn't get a robotic vacuum. She thinks it is unfair of him to expect his wife's mother to sweep up their crumbs.

"Have you read the news?" he asks.

"I try to avoid it," she tells him. "I don't like the negativity."

He tells her to google the robot vacuums. He is annoyed whenever she asks him a question that could be answered by the internet. But sometimes she likes extra words that stretch out a conversation, a face-to-face exchange of information.

"Is it so terrible to want to interact?" she asks.

"It's inefficient when you have information at your fingertips," he replies.

He picks up her phone and brings it to her, but she sets it back down.

"Just tell me," Bird says. "Stop being so infuriating."

He puts his fingers to his temples, annoyed. "The vacuums have hidden cameras that send videos to teenagers who strip out the nude scenes and sell the clips to porn sites." Bird is not sure if her brother is serious. She laughs to see if he will. He doesn't. She decides he is joking anyway. It is too horrifying to think he might not be.

"You have one?" he asks.

She nods.

"I don't think you will be able to find the clips," he says. "Your name won't be attached."

"But what if it is?" she asks. "I feel stupid."

He reaches for words to reassure her. "I try my best to avoid surveillance, but I drive an electric car. It knows more about me than my wife does. I can either pollute the planet or hand over my data. It's not a great choice, is it?"

Bird doesn't answer.

"My doctor's office sells my medical information to pharmaceutical companies," he continues. "I stream TV and get ads for Prozac. Just try to forget about it."

"Right," Bird says.

Later, after Royce retires for the evening, she pulls out her phone. She hopes he is messing with her, but an article in the *Times* confirms what he's said. The robots are equipped with hidden cameras. The company claims the video cameras are innocuous, used only to improve their products. There is no reference to porn sites, though there's an implication that the footage is sold to a third party.

She thinks back to the times she has undressed in front of her vacuum. She's often naked when she's alone. It has filmed every part of her.

WHEN VEE RETURNS TO her desk, the feed of the girl is gone. She doesn't know what's happened. It should be running all hours of the day. The vacuum knows how to charge itself. Later she realizes that the girl must have gotten rid of it. She feels guilty for spying on her.

Maybe Vee should have known better than to get involved with this job, but she needed it. She has become desensitized to the nude body. For weeks, hospital orderlies bathed and changed her. She hopes the girl is okay, but there is no way to check in on her. The girl is unaware of her existence, a thought that makes Vee sad.

The next morning, the feed switches to a lumberjack in a remote cabin. She quits her job, which makes her mother upset.

"How am I supposed to pay for your medical bills by myself?" she asks.

"Don't worry, I'll get a new job," Vee tells her. "A better one. I'll be racing again soon, anyway. I have plenty of money coming."

Her mother doesn't reply. She doesn't speak to her for the rest of the day. Vee doesn't know why. The silence feels like criticism, but later she hears her mother crying in her bedroom. She doesn't want to think about why her mother is in tears.

She remembers her sister's offer to let her move in, but the offer was extended with the understanding that Vee would soon be healthy. Her sister doesn't have time to look after her. And Vee doesn't want to distract her sister from her exams. But the real reason she doesn't want to live with her is that she feels she can't keep up the ruse. The fewer people Vee has to tell that she is disabled, the easier it will be for her to believe she has a normal future.

WHEN BIRD RETURNED TO Portland, she tossed the vacuum into the dumpster. Even with the vacuum gone, she was afraid to take off her clothes. She unplugged her microwave, her coffee maker, her toaster. She spent the next few days applying for jobs.

A few weeks later, she is offered a position at an art museum in Portland that doesn't have feely-box exhibits. Her new coworkers are welcoming, but Bird is unable to relax in their presence. One day she hears people giggling in the break room and thinks they are laughing at her. They look guilty when she says hi to them. She knows it is unlikely they will come across the nude footage of her, but she can't stop worrying. Every night she googles herself just in case the footage turns up. She looks for a new job that she can do from home.

She misses her brother. The visit to San Francisco was a bright spot in her year, but his wife is back home now and he doesn't have as much time for Bird. Another trip wouldn't help.

She watches his life unfold on Hearts. Usually he posts Jessica and the kids, but sometimes he posts street gum, abandoned stuffed animals, and the occasional picture of people wearing clothes that accidentally match the chairs they are sitting in. His posts have become bleaker in the days since her visit. His feed is now filled with overflowing trash cans, abandoned toilets, and the remnants of buildings that have burned down. There is nothing of his family.

One day Royce texts her a last-meal pastry. He never sends her texts—they only communicate on the app—so she knows the photo is significant. She googles Hearts, unprompted, and learns the app is shutting down within twenty-four hours.

She drives to San Francisco so she can be with him. By the time she arrives, the app no longer opens. Royce is sitting on the stoop with a coffee, his phone face down on the concrete. She tells him he'll make a new app. An even better one. Next time it will win. People will prize privacy again.

"Maybe people will quit social media," she says.

He laughs.

She thinks he will argue there's no going back now that people have been desensitized to data sharing, but he doesn't say anything.

They spend the morning joyriding through San Francisco, looking for people whose shirts match the murals behind them. Photos they would have posted.

THE GARBAGE PATCH

All Thuy wants is a man who will eat plastic with her, but it's been hard to find a man like that in this town. The rich guys pretend they are too good for it. She's given up on the idea of finding someone.

She is just hanging on. Her customer-service job is exhausting. She spends her day speaking to people who are angry their smart speakers aren't listening. Plastic is the only joy she has in her life, but the good kind is harder to come by. Scavengers pick up what they can find and sell it at a markup. She doesn't make enough to buy a steady supply. She has dreamed of visiting the garbage patch. There, she would have plenty of water bottles to chew on.

One day she decides to head out to the patch and calls in sick. She packs a flask, a snack, and sunscreen, but there are no boats available at the waterfront. Beecher's has rented out the fleet for a team bonding experience. The boats return in the afternoon, but she can feel the winds have changed.

She goes back to the kiosk the following morning, when the winds are more amenable. This time the proprietor tells her Uber has rented out the fleet. When she squints, she can see coders paddling over a swell. Tomorrow it'll be someone else.

THE NEXT WEEKEND, THUY takes a rideshare to the terminal north of the city and boards a ferry to Orcas Island. Her plan is to steal an emergency raft and row out to the patch, but when she gets to the lower deck where they're stored, there is already a willowy man in a Google tee standing near the only available raft. He looks to be in his thirties or forties. She's not sure. People can never guess her age either.

"Do you mind if we share this raft?" Thuy asks. "I need to get to the garbage patch."

Before the man can answer, she hops in.

"Hey, I was here first," the man says. "I have dibs on this raft."

His eye is twitching and he has a desperate look on his face. She knows that look.

"Are you going to the patch?" she asks.

The man in the Google shirt doesn't answer. Instead, he attempts to pick her up by the hips and toss her back onto the deck, but he has miscalculated her strength. He doesn't know she was an amateur boxer in her youth. It is not difficult for Thuy to break loose: One hard kick to his stomach, and the man is on his ass next to the raft.

The scuffle attracts the attention of the ferry security guard, who runs out from the main cabin with a large paddle. He threatens to whack them into the ocean if they don't vacate the raft.

"He's the one who wanted to steal it," Thuy tells the security guard. "I tried to stop him."

Security ignores her and hauls them both back onto the ferry, then handcuffs her to the man for the rest of the journey. They are shoved into a small room connected to the ferry's kitchen, where the hot dogs for the cafeteria are boiled.

"I am a pescatarian and this smell is offensive to me," the man in the Google shirt shouts dramatically, but Thuy is the only person who can hear him.

"Calm down," she says. "I don't want to end up in jail."

The man tries to sit down, but sitting requires Thuy's cooperation thanks to the handcuffs. They press their backs up against the wall opposite the kitchen equipment and lower themselves to the ground.

"Are they really going to leave us in here?" he asks. "There are no windows, no bathroom either. A jail cell would have a toilet at least."

"There's a bucket," she says. "I'll look away, if you must."

The man says he has never been treated so poorly in his life. Thuy isn't too happy about the situation either, but she can suffer through anything for an hour. A cafeteria worker comes in to retrieve the hot dogs, apologizing profusely for interrupting. She has mistaken them for lovers. She drops several steaming hot dogs into a basket and runs out of the room without looking at them. Then the ferry motor shuts off and the boat shudders. A few moments later, the security guard with the large paddle escorts them off the boat. He speaks to them as if they are one person.

"We don't need more crazies," he says. "No more ferries for you."

He walks them far from the dock, off the ferry-terminal property and down the road, before uncuffing them. Now she is stuck on an island with no way to get home.

"You smell like hot-dog skin," the man in the Google shirt complains.

"You think you smell good?" Thuy asks, crossing her arms.

"What if the smell never comes off?" the man asks. "What if we smell like this forever?"

"You're really neurotic, aren't you?" she says. "It's your fault we're stuck on this island."

"You shouldn't have jumped into my raft," the man says.

"We'll be much happier if we split up," she tells him. "I'll take this area. You can have the rest."

The man frowns. He appears to be unhappy seeing Thuy go, even though he has done nothing but complain about her. She walks a bit farther, then heads through the trees to a nearby beach, where there is a pretty view of the sound. She loosens her shoelaces and sticks her feet into what used to be sand. She remembers the days when beaches weren't made of ground-up trash. This thought makes her feel old.

She realizes just then that she is sitting near the summer

camp she attended in middle school. She hasn't thought about the place in years. She can hear children playing in the amphitheater in the woods, not far from the beach.

She walks over to see what it looks like now. The camp hasn't changed, but the children seem different, a glazed-over look in their eyes. She's heard on the news that children are given pills so that they will be productive. She thinks maybe it is for the best that these kids will never know what it is like to be sad. She can't remember the last time she felt content.

She has only a few friends—though they are more like strangers, work colleagues she sees over ramen and beer every few Fridays. They don't know what questions to ask one another, so they converse as if shouting into a void, with no regard to what was previously said. She misses her old boxing partners, who communicated with jabs. She prefers the taste of blood to the sound of bullshit. But they have moved on to cities where housing is cheaper. She is lucky she can manage with her salary.

Thuy watches the kids construct houses out of popsicle sticks. They are little worker bees, a neutral expression on their faces. They will grow up to be better members of society. If only her camp had dispensed those pills when she attended, perhaps she would have been the kind of daughter who made her parents proud. Perhaps she wouldn't have developed a taste for plastic.

Later in the afternoon she manages to convince a man in a crab boat to give her a ride home. The air smells like salt and clams. The rocking makes her feel calm like a baby again. She starts to worry she will never get to see the garbage patch.

* * *

THUY WORKS SO MANY hours the following week that she is too tired to scheme up a new way to the patch. There are many angry customers. But she can't complain, because she is no different from them. She is also a person who cannot be satisfied.

THE NEXT SATURDAY, THUY walks past an old art-house movie theater on her way to dinner. She has many memories of dates here, with artistic men who were too sensitive to write texts that made sense. They communicated in gibberish formatted like poetry, but at least there was a pleasing rhythm to their nonsense. Sometimes before bed she still pulls up their texts and reads them out loud until she is lulled to sleep.

Sorry, disappeared.
At the store with some seriousness
Aged gouda reminds me?
Too skinny, disappearing again.

The façade of the theater remains, though it hasn't screened a movie in a few years. Most of the small shops have shut down due to the cost of rent. She misses the days when her neighborhood wasn't full of empty shells of buildings, when Soundgarden spilled out of the windows. She hasn't eaten plastic in months, the longest stretch she can remember, but she decides to splurge today.

She arrives at the conveyor-belt sushi place down the street and eyes the water bottles—so many lined up on the counter, just waiting for someone to eat them. She has never seen anyone buy this many. Then she sees that the man in the Google shirt is sitting at the counter. These are his water bottles.

"It's you," the man says when she approaches.

"Yeah?" Thuy replies, shrugging.

The man stuffs a water bottle into his mouth and chews on it. He eats three more bottles, then serves himself two blue plates of sushi, then two red. He doesn't eat the most expensive ten-dollar yellow plates. His frugality intrigues her, but she tries not to let on that he has become interesting to her. She takes a seat next to him, then helps herself to a plate of inari, some pickled cucumbers, then eel. She orders only one water bottle. This is all she can afford. She chews on it slowly, hoping to make it last. The man smiles at her. His smile is awkward, unfinished, sort of like hers. He offers her a bottle from his stack.

"It's on me," he says. "Have as many as you please."

She wants to go crazy eating water bottles, but she takes just the one.

"I think we got off on the wrong foot," the man says. "We have some shared interests. Perhaps there is more common ground?"

She guesses they don't have much, given the discrepancy of their salaries. He can eat all the plastic he wants.

"Do you like music, movies, hiking?" he asks, as if they are all one thing.

She nods.

"I like movies," he says.

"My favorite theater closed down," she says. "The twin cinema up the hill. I miss it."

"I liked that place too," he says. "I saw *The Royal Tenenbaums* there once on a date. A fine film, though the date was weird. She expected me to pay for the movie tickets. Have you ever met a woman like that?"

Thuy shakes her head, though she is a woman like that. She thinks there is nothing wrong with chivalry; she longs for it, mostly because no date has ever bought her a gift. People think she is too tough to enjoy presents. They think she doesn't want to be the object of affection. It's true she hates flowers, but she would like a bouquet just once. Maybe she has a complicated demeanor that nobody quite understands, but she is a person with a soft spot.

The man in the Google shirt tucks a bib into his collar as if he suddenly means business. The logo on his shirt is now obscured. He tells her his name is Neil. He shoves another empty water bottle into his mouth and bites down hard. She closes her eyes and listens to the satisfying crinkle as he chews.

"I got into the stuff young," Neil tells her. "Mom says it was in the water. People looked down on her for letting me chew on it, but there was nothing she could do to keep the plastic out of my body. She figured I may as well enjoy it. She was being realistic."

"There's nothing wrong with plastic," she says. "It's human nature to want it. I wish my mother was more like yours."

"Maybe you'd like to catch a movie sometime?" Neil asks.

"I doubt we will be able to find a decent theater around here," she replies. The only one left is a big chain that screens the same movie on repeat. The entirety of the film is a single scene in which an unidentified monster stamps out all of Los Angeles. Thuy hasn't seen it, but she has no interest in movies without a good script. She prefers complex characters who make suffering seem attractive.

Neil pays for her water bottle, as promised. Thuy thinks maybe it would be nice to spend the evening out with him. She is enjoying the idea of being on a date. They walk over to the old art-house theater, now an empty brick building.

Neil presses his face to a window and narrates a movie to her. It takes her a few minutes to realize it's *Singles,* a film set in the neighborhood long ago. She remembers watching this movie in middle school. It didn't make an impression on her then, but now she likes the nostalgia of the city scenes. She longs for the time before the music venues were shuttered. She used to see a band nearly every night: Sleater-Kinney, Juno, Remy Zero, Sunny Day Real Estate. She misses the Coffee Messiah, the Sit & Spin, the ghosts of concerts past she still carries with her.

She feels a dreamy look sweep across her face. Neil thinks this look is meant for him and kisses her with his coarse cat tongue. She can taste the plastic in his mouth. She licks her lips until she starts to feel a buzz. Is this chemistry? she wonders. She has never felt chemistry with a man before, but now she can't stop kissing him. She realizes that she has real feelings for him. She had no idea what it felt like to be excited by someone. She thought she was too weird to be loved, but maybe she isn't.

* * *

IN THE MORNING, NEIL shows her his view of the garbage patch. It is impressive. His apartment has a prime view of the ocean.

"You're so lucky to have that view," Thuy says. "I would never leave my window."

Neil smiles. "You know, we could go to the patch together," he says. "I've thought about moving there, starting over."

"You can live at the patch?" she asks. She closes her eyes and imagines a life of all-you-can-eat plastic. No more feeling guilty about splurging on stuff she can't afford.

"We could get married there," Neil says.

"I can't imagine anything more romantic," she tells him.

She considers his proposal. It is crazy to elope, but there is nothing left for her in this city. Her friends are gone. She can't keep working at her dead-end job. She has felt less depressed since she met Neil. She could still visit her parents sometimes. She tells him she will marry him. This trip will be the beginning of her real life.

A FEW WEEKS LATER, Neil meets her at the pier. She brings only one suitcase, filling it with books and a few outfits. She hasn't told her parents she's eloping to the patch. She'd rather keep it uncomplicated. They would probably try to stop her, though they'd approve of Neil's job, so maybe they wouldn't.

Neil has rented a catamaran with a dining room and a large deck. Thuy is almost twitching from the anticipation of the plastic they will soon eat. He presses his cheek against hers and tells her the plastic will be all hers soon, that this is the life she deserves. He tells her she gives his life meaning. He had felt like an outcast before he met her, but now he doesn't have to crave plastic alone.

The journey to the patch takes two days on open water. It feels like an eternity. Before they arrive, she notices the water is shimmery and purple. Neil tells her they're sailing through microscopic beads of face wash. Soon she sees the first water bottle floating in the big blue ocean, and then a few more. Then suddenly they are right in the middle of the patch in all its garbage glory. It looks just like the pictures, bigger even. There are billions of plastic bottles floating among the fishing nets, barrels, and rope. She sees bits of plastic in every color. It catches the light in just the right way so that it sparkles. A beautiful sight, worthy of the cover of *National Geographic*.

The captain anchors the boat so they can go for a swim. Neil dives off the side and parts the water between a Frisbee and some flip-flops. Thuy leaps in after him, holding her knees to her chest. She never took swim lessons as a child and is lucky she can manage the waves with her head-above-water breaststroke. She inhales the therapeutic smell of trash and feels she has never been happier, except maybe once, at a Dinosaur Jr. show. Neil offers her an amuse-bouche of grocery bag, but she passes. She wants to see what else is out there. He splashes her and giggles.

"What are you giggling about?" she asks.

He pauses as if deciding whether to tell her what he is thinking.

"I love you more than plastic," he finally says.

"You're lying," she says playfully.

"Aren't you going to say it back?" Neil asks. "Do you love me too?"

"Of course I love you," she replies.

This is the best day of her life. She doesn't care that her arms are turning to jelly. There is plenty she can hold on to. Neil promises they will never leave—not unless she tires of it.

But she doesn't get to enjoy the garbage patch for the rest of her life. She doesn't even get to enjoy it for a full afternoon. She is chasing after a piece of purple LDPE when she swims into a dark abyss. She has no idea where she is—it looks like a small sea full of plastic bottles, a sea inside an ocean, a mini garbage patch.

She calls for Neil.

"You're in a whale," he explains. His voice sounds far away. "Try not to panic. I am working on getting you out. I have several Bitcoin."

"What is a whale doing at the garbage patch?" she calls back. She worries the whale has gotten lost.

Thuy is thrown about, and then there is a large splash from outside: The whale has flown out of the water and crashed back into the waves. Then it is steady—swimming, she thinks. She can hear the motor of the catamaran's dinghy. Neil must have leapt in to follow her. She hopes he has enough fuel to keep up. She hears him firing off flares and making loud calls to the Coast Guard. He shouts so she can hear how much work he is putting into rescuing her. Every time he lights a flare, the whale's stomach turns orange. She feels fine as long as she can hear Neil outside these walls, even if he is panicking. The inside of a whale isn't the worst place to spend time. It is kind of like glamping. She can wait for the Coast Guard to rescue her.

They swim along for a while. She loses track of time. She thinks she can see Neil through the whale's blubber but then decides maybe she is hallucinating because she's been inside for too long and it is dark and disorienting. She's reminded of the blur of her childhood spent with headphones on, a childhood that was lonely and disconnected. She was an only child with misfit parents who never talked to people. She is still unwinding being raised as a shut-in. She doesn't know what to say to strangers, so she usually keeps to herself. She'd never been on more than three dates with the same person until Neil. She feels lucky to have found him. She is almost a newlywed. If only she could get out of this whale.

She waits patiently, but the rescue team doesn't appear. Outside, Neil is apologizing profusely. He says he is calling his government connections because the Coast Guard got lost. The whale swallows a huge gulp of water along with a squid, a fish, and an octopus. She hadn't considered the possibility that Neil wouldn't be able to rescue her. He had seemed capable of anything. This was the quality she loved most about him. Can they have a good life with a whale in between them? How long will he follow her in his dinghy?

When she wakes up the next day, the motor sound is gone. She shouts that she loves him, but there is no response. She thinks maybe he has gone to get more fuel. He'll find her again. But what if he doesn't? What if the whale swims too far from the garbage patch and he loses track of her? What if there is only loneliness in her future? She doesn't know how to calm herself down, so she sits up against a whale wall and pretends that she is listening to music.

The whale senses her distress. He swallows several milk jugs. They come floating toward her, a gift. She will be okay without Neil, she thinks. The whale is a chivalrous guy. He will take care of her.

THE MILF HOTEL

I arrive in Madeira at four in the afternoon after a harrowing, windy landing. A black car greets me at the airport and shuttles me to the hotel. I've never been to Portugal. It's been a long time since I've traveled abroad—since before my son, Kirby, was born. The Portuguese sun makes me feel hopeful for the first time I can remember.

The car pulls up to the front of a modern glass hotel. I can see the ocean through the walls. Before I can enter the sliding glass doors, a producer escorts me around the side to a patio where the other contestants have gathered. He takes my phone, then hands me a tube of red lipstick and a champagne flute. I am wearing a Hole shirt and a sweater that is more like a bathrobe. I haven't brushed my hair. Grief is my stylist. I've brought my stuff in a trash bag instead of a purse.

"Welcome to the MILF Hotel," the producer says. "I think you're going to like it here."

I nod.

Several contestants stand with drinks near the pool bar. I meet Millicent, who is a food photographer, and Bonnie, who runs a wine shop in Scottsdale. They tell me they have lost their husbands in terrible accidents. I wouldn't have guessed it based on how put-together they look. Widows Who Glow, they call themselves. I'm jealous of them.

They introduce me to other Widows Who Glow: Myra, Tyra, Roxanne, Ethel, and Mimi. So many chipper women. I am the odd one out here.

I finish my champagne and look for another drink. By the bar I find someone who looks dull and angry. She says her name is Todd. That can't be her name, but it's what I hear when she introduces herself.

My husband was also named Todd. He was a pilot who died in a seaplane crash when Kirby was three. The investigator's report suggested he crashed on purpose. I didn't know Todd wanted to die. He'd kept a cheerful front. I never had time to process his death—the plunge into single motherhood was all-consuming. Todd was the one who wanted to have children so soon. He was nine years older than me. I wasn't prepared yet. I had just started my life. Every day was a sprint trying to keep Kirby alive. I didn't have time to join a grief group. My anxiety went unchecked. Every time I heard the house creak, I was convinced someone was breaking in. Once, when an old man lifted Kirby onto a swing at the park, I snatched my son out of his hands and shoved him away from us, convinced he was planning to run away with him. The world became a scary place after Todd died.

Kirby understood. As he grew older, he was the one who calmed me. He checked in often to reassure me he was alive while at a friend's house. In high school he lifted weights so he could protect us. I relied on him to make me feel safe. He soon slipped into the void Todd had left. We went out for burgers; we baked. He canceled plans with his friends so we could go to concerts. We were together every hour he wasn't at school. Then he decided to attend college far away at McGill instead of the University of Washington. The last-minute switch hurt me deeply. He said he needed space. He didn't call much. After sharing a life for eighteen years, we were practically estranged.

Before he left, he suggested that I try dating, so I joined an app for the widowed. The men I met spoke of their wives as if they were alive. I couldn't shake the feeling that we were cheating on dead people, especially when my dates called me by the wrong name over appetizers. I needed to be around happy people. I started to think the key to success lay in dating younger men. Men who had yet to be scarred. Men who had Kirby's energy.

"I'm sorry about your husband," the lady Todd says, resting her head on my arm.

"Thank you," I say.

Across the patio, Ethel and Bonnie erupt into laughter. The lady Todd and I exchange a look. "Happy people are weird," she says. "Fake," she says, with a wink. She suggests we form an alliance as the sane ones. I nod, relieved to have a friend here. She returns to the bar to get another drink.

One last contestant enters the patio. She is on her phone,

doing business. She looks younger than the rest of us—late twenties. She says her name is Cutty and she is the founder of an app that redistributes food and supplies to needy people. She wears shoes that are smaller than her feet. She is the only one among us who hasn't lost a husband. She adopted her son from an orphanage in Malawi. Roxanne and Mimi exchange looks. They don't think Cutty should be here. I don't either. Then I realize she has likely been cast to cause conflict. I adjust what is probably a bitchy look on my face as the cameras whip toward me. I'll have to work hard to keep my face neutral.

A man who is scratching his hair approaches me. He seems to be in a hurry. He says we need to do the shot. At first I think he means we need to film the intro. I tell him I'm not ready yet, but he pulls out a syringe and rolls up my sleeve before I can ask questions. The injection feels like a small pinch. My eyes roll back in my head for a moment. I feel someone's arms grasping me just as I start to tip over. I am not sure how long I'm out, but when I come to, I feel lighter.

"What was in that syringe?" I ask him.

"Your youth," he says. I decide that I'm fine with the shot. I've come on this show to have a new experience. I am tired of my routine. They can do whatever they want to my body.

He hands me a key and escorts me to my fifth-floor room. It's spacious, with an ocean view and a heart-shaped sofa, every bit of it tastefully designed. I rest my fingertips on the windowsill. There's an Olympic-sized pool just below. Maybe I do feel a little more relaxed when I see the view. The man tells me that I will have plenty of time to swim while I'm here. He hangs a zebra-striped bikini and matching silk robe on the bathroom door. For later.

LATER, IN MY HOTEL room, I prepare for a scene. The hair and makeup artist, Yawny, sticks her hands in my hair and gets a feel for it, then brushes it out. She tells me she thinks I'll win the competition. She says I have an interesting face.

"You normally date younger men?" she asks.

"No, never," I say.

She puts my hair in rollers but decides I don't have enough volume, so she opts for a full wig. It looks how my hair used to look when I met Todd—voluminous, halfway down my back. Then she pulls out a large tube of concealer and sets to work under my eyes.

"Time stopped when your husband died," she says. "You think you're the age of the boys you're going to meet."

"Is that my problem?" I ask. "How do I get unstuck?"

"You have to believe the future will be as good as the past," she replies.

I have no idea what she means. It seems impossible to imagine a future that could rival the life I have lost. Picnics with Todd, and then later with Kirby. We had Kidd Valley milkshakes in the car between his doubleheaders. We listened to Fiona Apple before bed. He knew all the words.

"You rely on your son too much," Yawny says.

"Maybe," I say.

By the time Yawny finishes painting on my left eyebrow, I look like the person I was twenty years ago, before anything terrible happened to me. I step into my dress and make my way down to the bar. The cameras follow me as I enter.

The women line up on one end of the room. Everyone looks younger than they did earlier. The men are behind a large red velvet curtain on the other side. A waitress in a sequined bra is passing out tall glasses of pastis. I take one and feel the effects of the alcohol after just a few sips. I can feel myself wobbling a little bit. I've had too much to drink and I'm not used to heels at this age.

I find the lady Todd. We are dressed in similar loud shoulder-padded dresses. *Twins,* she mouths. I give her a thumbs-up. The other women giggle nervously as we wait. A waitress hits a gong. The curtain is lifted. The boys are revealed. They are dressed in matching white jumpsuits. Nine young hopeful faces take us in, but ten of us look back. We will have to fight for them. I scan their faces as I try to come up with a plan of attack. One looks a bit like my son. I avoid making eye contact with the Kirby look-alike and search for someone to make out with.

The lady Todd breaks the ice first, kissing the boy who is closest to her. The rest of us laugh. Then a boy with a buzz cut walks toward me and buys me a drink. He says his name is Tiny. He's twenty-one. He has an accent I can't place—maybe a Boston one. He says I look interesting. He asks me why I'm doing the show. I tell him I needed a little spark to get me going again.

"What's your story?" I ask, leaning in.

"I'm a magician," he says. "Want to have some fun tonight? I can show you some tricks."

He is just odd enough to pique my interest. I hold his hand and run out of the bar, down the hall toward his room, unsure if we are going to do magic tricks or have sex. I'm fine with either outcome. When we enter his room, he tells me to wait a minute, then pulls out a red velvet pouch from his bedside drawer. A kidney-like object tumbles out into his palm. He says it is his magic bean. It shoots out of his ear and suddenly it's between two of his toes. Then I feel it stuck between my ribs and inside my throat before it pops out of my mouth and lands back in his hand.

"That's really cool," I tell him. "How did you do that?"

"It's magic," he whispers.

IN THE MORNING, I wake up in Tiny's bed. I feel hungover. A little dry and dirty, but in a good way. His skinny, crooked arm is draped across my waist. I set my head on his chest. We stay cuddling until a producer knocks on our door and tells us it's time for breakfast. Tiny zips up his white jumpsuit. I put on yesterday's dress and walk arm in arm with him down to the breakfast buffet. As we exit the elevator, Yawny intercepts me. She pulls me into a bathroom.

"We need to touch you up first," she says.

I watch as she paints on a new coat of my young face. She straightens out the wig next. It felt odd when she first put it on, but now I can't imagine myself without it.

"How did it go last night?" she asks.

I smile.

"You're glowing," she says, nodding. "It's good to see you so happy."

"I never thought I could be a Widow Who Glows," I tell her.

"You're surprising yourself," she replies. "Good for you. Not everyone has a good time on these shows."

"Really?" I ask. "It's a free vacation to Portugal."

"It doesn't always feel like a vacation," she says.

After she puts on my red lipstick, she says I look stunning. By the time I emerge from the restroom, the other couples have already arrived and they're sitting together at tables outside. Millicent is tucking her boy's napkin into his shirt. Mimi is brushing her boy's hair. There are twenty different kinds of cheeses on the table. Fruit of every color. I hand Tiny a glass of orange juice and sit down next to him. He blushes.

"You're so beautiful," he says.

I enjoy making him blush. He plays footsie with me under the table while we eat.

ON DAY TWO, WE are allowed out of the hotel for the first time. We can go wherever we want. Tiny and I spend a few hours walking around Funchal, wandering through the old center square, where people in felt hats weave clothes for small children. Cats lick our ankles. Merchants peddle loaves of bread. We cross paths with an elderly British couple trekking through the square in search of a trailhead. I am jealous they've made it this far without suffering a terrible accident. Tiny says they could be us one day, but then he realizes that I am thinking about my husband and not him.

He asks me what Todd was like. I tell him he flew us out to remote landing strips in the mountains for dates. We would hike up hidden trails and arrive back home in time for dinner. The day we got married, he gave me an atlas of unusual islands and said we were going to visit all of them. We went to Easter Island on our honeymoon. Madeira was not on the list, but Todd would have enjoyed it here, and not just for the terrifying landing. He liked a good aviation challenge. I feel guilty that I am experiencing this beautiful island without him. The grief makes my nerves feel like strings that have been plucked. It's like a low rumbling in my stomach, a tiny horror movie that plays out only inside my body. The orchestra of my nervous system. The mountains are enshrouded in a soft fog. This island is beautiful. I need to pull myself together and enjoy my time here.

"How did he die?" Tiny asks.

I tell him he had an unexpected accident.

"I lost someone like that too," Tiny says.

He doesn't tell me who, though I have some guesses.

After lunch, we go on a hike and run into the others. Roxanne and Bonnie are trying to keep up with their boys. Tyra walks alone. She is the odd one out. I am grateful I'm not her. Cutty is carrying hers on her shoulders. I hike faster so Tiny will think I'm strong. By the time I get to the top, I'm exhausted. There is no view because the fog is so thick, but Tiny says it's better this way. Romantic. He walks closer to the edge of a cliff to look at the view, but I worry he is going to fall off the side. I shout for him to stop, and he looks back at me, startled.

"I'm not going to fall," he assures me.

"Sorry," I tell him. "I worry too much. I'm nuts, you know. I twitch all night in my sleep like a cat."

"I don't know if you've noticed," he says. "But everyone here is nuts. No one sane would sign up for a dating show."

"You too?" I ask him.

He winks, then shoots his bean out of his belly button. I take a deep breath and compose myself. There's no reason to be anxious here. I notice Tiny's shoulders are getting red.

"You're burning up," I tell him. "You need sunscreen."

I pull a tube out of my backpack and rub the lotion into his skin, and he lets out a sigh of pleasure.

DAY THREE: TINY WHISPERS good morning and brushes my hair back from my face. We have feverish sex, and afterward I fall out of bed with joy. I literally roll over expecting there to be more bed. Tiny laughs and helps me back up onto it, but just as we start kissing again, it's time for breakfast.

"I wish we could order room service," he says.

"I like the spread," I say. "When I go back home, I'm going to start every day with a buffet. I'll set out croissants, twenty kinds of cheese, pastries, jam, and eggs on my table. A buffet for one."

"For two," he says, pulling me closer. "I'm coming to visit you in Washington. I have three weeks off for winter break."

"That sounds fun," I tell him. "Three weeks of being rained in."

"We don't need to go outside," Tiny says, winking. Then I remember that Kirby is supposed to visit during the holiday. We had plans to see *The Nutcracker*. The idea of him meeting Tiny repulses me. Then I think maybe it could be nice to have both of them under the same roof. The situation would be delicate, but perhaps I could find a way to manage it.

I decide to stop by my room on my way to the buffet. I want to take a quick shower first and freshen up. My good mood dissipates when I emerge from the shower and see my face in the mirror. Now that the makeup has washed off, there are severe lines at the corners of my eyes. Fat clumps are stuck to weird parts of my cheeks. It's better when I don't smile. I lift my wig and see that my hair has grayed. It's not just a few streaks. There's nothing black left. I look like I've aged twenty years since arriving in Madeira.

I hide behind a newspaper and walk through the hotel, looking for Yawny. I find her over by the bar and ask what happened to my face. She seems surprised I don't know. She tells me that by appearing on the show and accepting the beauty treatments, I had agreed to surrender the last of my youth. I must have missed that part of my contract.

"This is messed up," I tell her. "Was it the shot? What was in that syringe?"

"Don't worry," she says. "You look great with the show makeup on. Better than you did before."

"What happens when I go home?" I ask.

"Just keep the wig on," she says, shrugging.

"I don't want to keep the wig on," I say. "I want my hair back."

After she finishes up, I walk over to the pool. I find the lady Todd in a lounge chair at the corner by the bar. She is sipping an Aperol spritz. She gestures down at Cutty, who is swimming laps.

"I used to be like that," the lady Todd says. "I worked out three hours a day. I wouldn't go on vacation because I was scared to miss a day of exercise. I'd walk several miles to get drinks with my friends. I could never walk enough. But it all catches up to you. Can't keep exercising forever. At some point you have to confront the rotten stuff inside."

I nod, then realize I have no idea what she means.

"What rotten stuff?" I ask.

"I shouldn't get into it," she says. Her comment leaves me intrigued. I want to know what rotten stuff is inside her.

After the cameras move away, I lean in closer to her.

"Has anything strange happened to you here?" I ask in a low voice.

She lifts her wig and flashes her gray. I show her my hair, the same shade.

"Oh no," she says. She says she saw Tiny talking to the hotel staff earlier. She says she's still trying to put it together, but she suspects the boys work for the hotel.

"Is Tiny making me old?" I ask, patting my hair.

"Maybe," she says. "I'd keep a distance."

"This place is getting weird," I say.

She nods.

"We have to get out of here," she says. She stands up and I follow her.

We head to the hotel lobby and try to exit through the front, but the glass doors don't open. The receptionist doesn't acknowledge us. She is busy helping someone else. She ignores me even as I shout. Next we try exiting the hotel at the back by the pool, but there is a tall fence surrounding the perimeter. I look for a spot where I can hop it, but the hedges are too tall. We will have to make a scene of it. I push a trash bin over by a part of the hedge that is farthest from the hotel. Before I can hoist myself on top of this can, a pool boy escorts us back to our rooms.

Once he leaves, I run down the hallway in search of a side door, but all of them are locked. I try the next floor up, but the emergency exits are also locked there. There is no way out of the hotel. I'm a prisoner here. The panic sets in. What if I never see Kirby again? What if I die here? I head back toward the elevator to regroup.

As I head down the long and narrow carpeted hallway, I see Tiny rounding the corner. I pretend I don't see him and keep going, but he catches up to me just as an elevator arrives. I step in, but he puts his hand inside before I can close the door on him.

"Are you okay?" he asks.

I nod. Something about his voice is off. I start to think his Boston accent is fake.

"You've been acting kind of weird," he says.

"I have a migraine," I tell him, rubbing my head.

"Did I do something wrong?" he asks.

"I need space," I say.

I ask where his magic bean is. I want to keep away from it. He shoots it out of his belly button at me. I catch it without thinking, then drop it on the elevator floor, worrying this bean has cast a spell on me. I smash it with my foot so it can't age me. The bean is misshapen now. It looks like a dead bug. Tiny stares at it in shock. Then he kneels down and tries to scrape it off the carpet. The door closes behind him, and the elevator takes us to my floor.

"I don't think it can do magic anymore," he says.

"I'm sorry," I say.

I can see pieces of the bean stuck under his fingernail.

"I'll have to cancel my tour," he says. "Did you do that on purpose?"

"Of course not," I say.

I hold my breath until the elevator doors open again.

Then I hurry off to my room. He doesn't follow this time. He is crying over his magic bean. I can hear the whimpering until the elevator door closes.

Back in my room, I check my hair to see if being around him has aged me. It looks about as gray as it did this morning.

I call Yawny and tell her I want to quit. She warns me that I can't go home until after the filming is over. The eliminated contestants are exiled on a boat to avoid spoilers. When I protest, she says sequestering is common on elimination shows. Otherwise, people would be able to deduce the finalists. I had forgotten about the boat. I imagine being thrown about in a tiny windowless room. I get seasick easily. If I quit, I will be swapping one form of imprisonment for another. I can't live for months on a boat.

I run to the lobby and demand to be let out. This time the receptionist releases the doors. I don't believe they are open at first. I stare at the plants just outside the hotel, but as the doors start to close again, I sprint out into the sunny world and hail a taxi to the airport. I catch the next flight home and try not to worry about how much it costs.

IN THE MORNING, I stumble out of bed and see a ball of fur on my lamp. At first I scream, thinking there is an animal in my room. Then I remember I had tossed off my wig in the dark last night. It must have landed here.

I had thought I'd feel safe once I was back home, but I don't. The same unsettling feeling has followed me here. As I brush my teeth, I keep an eye out behind me in the mirror. I worry a producer will appear and drag me back to the show or, even worse, out onto the boat. But there is a scarier image I can't escape: my own face. The gray hair seems to change the shape of my head. It makes the skin look thinner, the head smaller. This is not the person I was when I met Todd. This is not the person who raised Kirby. I have paid a price for a small bit of fun.

I put the wig on and feel the life coursing through me. I feel virile. I feel like someone who would drink V8 juice. The wig is my superpower, though it is only a temporary salve that also depletes me.

THE NEXT MORNING, I make myself a cup of coffee. I drink it with milk and sugar, the way Todd took it. I do this despite hating the taste of most sugar. Then I call Kirby and tell him that I've returned from a trip. He sounds busy and says he didn't realize I had gone anywhere.

"You really didn't notice I was gone?" I asked.

"Nope," he says.

I remind myself a week isn't long. It's just that the week had felt like months.

"You're allowed to go on vacation, Mom," he says, laughing. "I don't know why you're shocked. I don't need you to check in on me that often."

"I want to know someone would notice if I slipped in the tub," I say. "That's all. I do live alone."

"I'll see you at Christmas," he says cheerfully.

"Anything special you want to eat?" I ask.

"I like all of your food," he says.

"Then I'll make all of it," I say. "It's good you're coming for two weeks."

He says has to go. He has a study group for his physics midterm.

I think about how, when Kirby was younger, I'd been desperate for time to myself. I'd never had a chance to see what I could do after marrying young. I had wanted to get my pilot's license, but there was never any time. I'd gone all-in on parenting my son.

It's chilly in Washington. I curl up in bed with a book to get warm, but I can't relax. I want to fix whatever is wrong. I need to patch up the hole inside me or the rotten stuff will come oozing out. I enter my closet, which looks like a time capsule from before Todd died. The hangers are filled with my old, bright mid-century modern dresses and Todd's clothes. I had kept them so I could smell his scent, as if he were an animal.

I pull out some of his clothes and bring them to bed with me: a flannel shirt and a pair of jeans that look bright despite their age. From the dresser, I grab his leather aviator hat. He had two. His smell is long gone, but the sight of the clothes is comforting. I can almost see his long legs and long neck. Bits of our conversations drift back to me.

"How does a giraffe fit into a cockpit?" I used to ask. He had seemed to shrink himself to get inside.

"I had to make it work," he'd say. "What's the alternative? Stay home? Do nothing? Get a nine-to-five? Sit at a desk?"

Flying wasn't a practical dream for a giant, but he wasn't going to give up on what he wanted just because he barely fit inside a cockpit. There was a drive about him that I had never seen in anyone else. He had known at age ten that he would fly planes. When had he known he would kill himself? Was it after I got pregnant? After I gave birth and underwent a metamorphosis into motherhood? Did he want to die before he met me? Did I stumble into a life that was already on its inevitable trajectory, or did I send him on it?

I fall asleep awkwardly next to Todd's clothes and wake up with a stiff back that has me hunched over for the rest of the morning.

I CALL KIRBY WITH increasing frequency as his holiday visit approaches. I do some shopping. I wrap his presents as soon as I buy them. I buy the Shrinky Dinks we'd made when he was a kid, thinking he might get a kick out of them.

While I am out running errands, I see a billboard advertising the premiere of my show. I blush, thinking of Kirby seeing my scenes with Tiny, yet I can't bring myself to warn him.

He calls me a few hours later, but he doesn't mention the show. Instead, he tells me that he's thinking of switching his major to philosophy.

"Why would you do that?" I ask. "Did you fail the test?"

"Of course not," he says. He's always had a good head on his shoulders. He had entered college wanting to be an engineer. He'd never mentioned an interest in the humanities.

"Can you get a job with that degree?" I ask.

"Of course you can," he says. "Philosophy majors do well on the LSAT. Better than anyone else."

"Oh, that's good," I say. "I imagined you would discuss the meaning of life."

"I take classes on logic and linguistics," he tells me. "And anyway, I'm an existentialist."

"I see," I say, though I don't see. I feel preoccupied with the fact that the show is about to premiere. I wonder if he has seen the billboard. "You're not mad at me, are you?" I ask.

"No," he says. "Why would I be?"

Later that night, there is a commercial that runs to promote the show. It consists of a clip of me tickling Tiny and him laughing hysterically for twenty seconds. Nothing else. Then the title comes on the screen with the tune-in information.

A FEW DAYS LATER, I watch the show alone in my pajamas. The series opens with the MILF meet-and-greet outside the hotel. I am escorted in by a producer who appears on camera. I had mistakenly gotten the impression this cocktail hour was not part of the show. The person on the screen is both me and not me. It is some approximation, with words chopped out from my speech. I am a fish out of water, made to look quirky among the other women. But I can't put the blame solely on the editing. The trash-bag purse doesn't help. I had stopped looking after myself. The Widows Who Glow annoy me as much as they did in person. As we drink and awkwardly chat about our deceased husbands, the score conveys a *Lord of the Flies* vibe, with a drumbeat that is suggestive of cannibalism. Many of the shots are taken by overhead drones that make us look like specks.

At least Tiny and I get a nice edit. He looks so friendly

that I find it hard to believe I was afraid of him. Who wouldn't want to cuddle with a cute little boy like him? We are the feel-good couple that everyone is rooting for. We don't spend our time trying to scheme others off the show. We get lost in being kids again. It's good between us, until he shoots his bean at me and I crumple in fear.

The episode ends with security-camera footage of me fleeing the hotel and Tiny being pulled away from his smashed magic bean. The show breaks the fourth wall, revealing producers who pry Tiny out of the elevator and coax him to move on to a new MILF.

KIRBY GOES SILENT AFTER the premiere airs. I fear the worst—that he will never speak to me again. He answers the phone again after a couple of weeks and doesn't mention the show, though he sounds rushed and says he has only a few minutes to talk. He tells me there is an update. He has met someone. A few days ago he dropped his keys in a toilet at a party, and an attractive woman had fished them out for him.

"She sounds like a keeper," I tell him.

"She is," he says. "We're going out again tomorrow night."

"That's great," I say. I force myself to sound happy for him.

It's difficult to adjust to the idea of Kirby having a girlfriend. He's never dated anyone. He didn't have a father figure to show him how to love someone. It feels odd that he could love someone else. This news complicates his upcoming visit for me emotionally. Will he spend his entire visit wishing he was with her? I decide I'm being ridiculous. There is room in his heart for both of us. I don't need to feel pinched.

THE DAY THAT KIRBY is due to arrive for Christmas break, I wear my favorite orange dress.

When I pick him up at the airport, he is standing on the curb in a smart aviator jacket. He looks much older than I remember. The wiry, athletic, nerdy body is gone. He has thickened and grown a mustache. He looks closer to Todd than to Todd's kid. He has Todd's bushy eyebrows and sharp chin. He expresses surprise that I am wearing a dress when I hop out of the car to hug him.

"You look good," he says.

"Thanks," I tell him. "I'm making some changes. No more feeling sorry for myself."

"Good!" he says. "I knew you would be happier once I left and you were forced to make friends."

I don't tell him I haven't made friends. I take his luggage and load it into the car, wobbling in my stilettos. I no longer have the ankle strength to wear heels. When we get home, he avoids my gaze as he sits down on the couch. Here it comes. He is going to tell me I am a terrible person for tickling a twenty-one-year-old kid.

"I can't stay that long," he says. "I need to go back on Saturday."

"Why?" I ask. "I thought we were doing New Year's. Ball drop, cheese plate, Martinelli's. Real booze?"

"Lisa and I have plans," he says. I figure Lisa is the Toilet

Bowl Girl. "We're hosting a dinner party together. Our first. Three couples are coming."

My worst fears are happening. He has less time to spend with me.

"I paid for your flight," I say.

"I'll pay you back," he says, shrugging. "Anyway, I already called the airline."

"Invite her to come here," I say.

"We haven't been together long," he says. "Maybe once we get more comfortable."

"You seem comfortable," I say.

"We're not," he says. "That's why I'm going back. To seal the deal."

I ask if he is hungry. He says he is.

I put on an apron and fry him egg rolls, his favorite dish. The house smells of oil, a smell that I love. He says he missed my cooking. It is the one thing he can't get in college. As if it's not my companionship he's interested in but rather what I can do for him. I vaguely remember feeling unappreciated by Todd, but my memory is hazy because I've buried everything I disliked about him. It doesn't feel right to think about fights with a spouse who isn't here to defend himself. I prefer to hold on to the good parts.

"What does Lisa cook?" I ask.

"I don't know," he says. "We haven't planned the menu yet." He reminds me they eat cafeteria food in their dormitories. This dinner party is a project they are embarking on together. They are excited to go to a grocery store to pick out cheese and wine.

Then Kirby turns to me and tells me he didn't watch the

show but Lisa did. So did his friends. It was a topic of conversation in his dormitory, which was something I had feared. The boys joked about wanting to come home to meet me, as if I would date them too.

"I hope you defended me," I say. "Did you tell them I'm not a MILF?"

He says Lisa had done some damage control, but he's still afraid to be alone around his friends.

"I'm not a MILF," I repeat.

"Why would you do a show like that?" he asks. "It's embarrassing."

"It was a mistake," I say. "I was having a midlife crisis, but that's over now. I'm not going to be dating college boys. Let's talk about something else. I want to hear more about Lisa. Can I see a photo of her?"

He pulls his phone out and scrolls through an album. Finally she comes into view. She has thin red hair, black plastic glasses, and a shapely bottom.

"You look cute together," I say. "Maybe you should tell me more about her. You are young, after all. You might be rushing it."

"I already know she's my other half," he says.

"How?" I ask.

He tells me they both like traveling. There's so much of the world they have yet to see. He says that they plan to go to Tokyo next summer. For spring break, they will go to Medellín. I tell him that Todd and I also fell in love while traveling.

"You don't know enough about your father," I say, after I get some wine in me. "We need to amend that." He nods. He rarely asked questions about Todd while growing up. I was too ashamed to speak about him. I show him photos of Todd with his plane. He seems surprised we flew somewhere new every weekend. He has only been on large jets. He has seen some far-flung cities, but he has never picnicked in the wilderness.

"I don't know if I have the courage to get in a Cessna," Kirby says, after taking in these photos. "Those planes crash all the time. Lisa's sister's family died in a seaplane. Delia, her husband, their son, and their unborn child. It was a maintenance issue." Then he looks right into my eyes. "What are the odds that both of us lost family members to plane crashes that were due to mechanical error?"

He still thinks Todd's death was an accident. I don't tell him it was an error of a different sort. I don't tell him his father had practiced the route in his flight simulator, which left no doubt of his intentions. I don't tell him that I never suspected anything was off. I'd thought we had a good life together. His melancholy streak was so small that it only appeared on the gloomiest of days, when anyone would be depressed.

Looking at these photos, I think Kirby is right. I must have been crazy to climb into a stranger's Cessna, but Todd had assured me that any aircraft was as safe as the pilot flying it.

AFTER KIRBY RETURNS TO Montreal, I watch the next installment of the show. I have left the hotel, but Tiny still talks about me with the lady Todd. He is unable to make sense of why I suddenly withdrew from him. The lady Todd doesn't mention that she warned me about the boys. She doesn't seem scared of him. The drum score intensifies as they share a kiss and he climbs into bed next to her. He looks comforted in her arms and sucks on his thumb. The sight of them curled up together makes me realize we have made a mistake.

From here, the camera zooms out until it is outside the walls and hovering over the hotel, where it pauses for a moment before zooming out so far that I see all of Madeira, the Earth, and the Milky Way. The camera work gives me the impression that there is nothing that does not fall under the scope of the show. This makes sense. Kirby doesn't remember a world before reality television existed. He came of age during the erosion of truth, when false narratives could easily take root.

I can't look away from the screen. I search for the boundaries of the show so I can exit it, but the camera never zooms in. As credits roll over the shot of the galaxy, I hear the drum music beating inside me.

THE CLOUD

No one warns me that I will lose my body parts during the blackouts. The first time the power goes out, my arm fades away. When I call the Southern California Electric Company, the customer-service representative tells me not to worry—my arm is safe in "the cloud."

"So it's coming back?" I ask impatiently.

"That's the idea," she says.

I don't have time to investigate further. My toddler, Ondine, is tugging at my leg. She doesn't care that my arm is missing. She doesn't care that the power is out. I have spent too much time on the phone asking about my arm; my daughter is melting down.

She is naked because it is too hot for clothes. It is 110 degrees. We are on our fourth day of a punishing heat wave. The utility company has shut off power preemptively because they don't want to get sued for causing another fire. Their infrastructure is aging, and this is their only way to deal with it. My husband, Edgar, goes down to the basement looking for matches and flashlights for what seems like six hours but is probably only five minutes. I imagine he is sitting on the bottom step, huddled over his phone, reading baseball scores on Twitter—avoiding Ondine's screams and using up his precious battery.

He needs breaks. He works all week straightening doors that have gone crooked. Doors that look like they were drawn by cartoonists. The ground shifts often in Los Angeles, thanks to the extreme temperature swings and the clay soil. The swings are more severe now than they've ever been.

Ondine is hungry. Somehow I rummage through the pantry in the dark, without my arm. As soon as I find the can opener, I realize I need my husband's help. He reemerges later and opens three cans of emergency supplies. We eat cold soup for dinner. This is the least our daughter has ever complained about a meal.

We spend the rest of the evening trying to keep her entertained. If only the electricity worked. It's only once we get her to bed that I have time to worry about my arm again. What if I can't take care of Ondine? What if more parts go missing? What if I end up just a stem? All my limbs ripped off me?

The power is still out when Ondine wakes up. My husband decides to take her for a walk in the early morning before it gets too hot. He senses I could use some alone time. It's snowing ash flakes outside.

There is nothing I want more than time to search for my arm, but I worry about the air quality. He says a little ash won't kill her. I should prioritize myself. They won't be gone for too long. As they step outside, a few flakes land in her hair. It looks beautiful. I think of a photo of me as a child, standing at a picnic area in Mount Rainier, with snowflakes in my braids, clutching a snowball, grinning. I got to breathe clean air as a child. I haven't done as well for Ondine. I try not to think about the world she will inherit. But there is an orange hue on the wall from the sky, and it is impossible to turn away from whatever is happening outside.

I call customer service frantically, shrugging the phone between my neck and my shoulder so I can have my one hand free. The phone menu is a labyrinth that leads me back to the beginning. It wasn't this hard to get through yesterday. They must be getting too many calls. I try to make peace with having one arm. Maybe I don't need it. Of course I need it. I am lying to myself. I've grown too used to rolling with the punches ever since becoming a mother.

The last time life felt normal, I was nearly eight months pregnant. I had just produced my last show—a docuseries about six Brazilian friends who couldn't get along. The show was a comedy, but it had turned into a drama in its fifth season, after an explosive fight ended the core friendships in real life. I was looking forward to taking some time off to look after my soon-to-be-born daughter. I thought we would be beginning a joyful chapter. Then I started getting strange headaches. My OB diagnosed me with severe preeclampsia and admitted me directly to the hospital. She feared that my brain was swelling.

I was put on a magnesium drip to ensure I didn't have a stroke or a seizure. The medication made my legs wobbly and my vision blurry. I developed numb patches all over my face. The neurologists became concerned I had developed MS. I was forced to wait until after the birth before they could investigate.

The delivery was the smoothest part of the experience. Ondine came out in four easy pushes, then she was alive—pristine, as if she hadn't just exited a body. She was healthy enough that she didn't need extra medical attention. I was the one who was still waiting to find out my fate. I worried I'd be paralyzed. It was easy to imagine how this would feel; I'd already spent two days on an epidural, being turned in my bed by nurses, propped up by pillows.

Edgar was so scared about me that he spent most of his time pacing the hospital corridors outside my room. Luckily, my MRI came back clear. The numb spots were chalked up to atypical migraines. We thought the hardest times were behind us, but a few months after we brought Ondine home, the wildfires erupted, and soon we had to contend with blackouts.

I've heard of friends having mental breakdowns after becoming mothers. People see shrimp crawling up their bathroom walls. Tiny ninjas run across their bedrooms. But I'm not the one having a breakdown. It's the world around me that's breaking down. At least I'm not in pain. There is no wound. It is as if my arm never existed. I don't have to tend to it. I don't have to go to the hospital. I am free to move on with the chores of the day.

The next morning, while I'm in bed, the lights finally come on. My arm reappears at my side. I wave it to make sure it is still connected. It's buzzing a little bit, like the nerves are talking to the grid. Electricity flows in and out of the wrong places. The buzzing continues as I work through my morning chores. It's distracting, uncomfortable, strange.

A COUPLE OF WEEKS later, the next time the lights flicker, my leg disappears. It leaves my body just as our house goes dark. "This again," I shout. Edgar frowns. I try to tell him I am scared, but he doesn't hear me. He's busy fiddling with the electric panel, as if we've just blown a fuse and my leg will reset.

It's harder to get tasks done without a leg. Ondine demands that I carry her around the house. She is capable of walking, but she doesn't want to walk. She won't let Edgar carry her, either, so he carries me while I carry her.

"Just let me know where you need to go," he says. "I'll be your legs."

By evening his helpful mood is gone. He complains his back hurts. He is concerned about missing too much work. We don't get paid if he doesn't work.

"When is your leg coming back?" he asks. "We need it."

I frown. He has said the wrong thing.

"So it's a family leg now," I say.

He nods. I want to tell him that I'm scared. That I'm a person who needs support. I want him to comfort me and tell me that I'll be whole again, but he's so busy tending to Ondine that there isn't much left in his tank for me.

At least it's not so hot this time. Only 96 and not 110—

a reasonable temperature for a hot day in Los Angeles. I try not to think about the fact that we could be comfortable if the utility companies had maintained their shoddy equipment.

After Edgar puts Ondine in her crib, he joins me in bed.

"Why are they doing this to me?" I ask.

"They need money," he guesses. He points out that the utility companies are in trouble after the lawsuits from last year's fires.

"But why didn't they take your leg?" I ask. "Why mine?"

"I don't know," he says. "But it's good one of us is healthy. Imagine if neither of us could work. Who would pay our bills?"

I have trouble sleeping. Then Ondine wakes up crying. At breakfast, she throws her cup against the wall. Then she begs for it back. Edgar brings her the cup, but it doesn't help. She throws it again and screams louder. There's nothing we can do to calm her down. I tell him not to reward her behavior. He tells me that he's looking after her and I should let him handle it. She is acting out because we are stressed.

The power comes back on the next morning. My leg returns. I retrieve Ondine from the crib and feed her breakfast.

"It's good to see you moving again," Edgar says.

"I know," I say. There's no worse feeling than not being able to take care of my child. I am free to move on with the chores of the day. I should feel happy, but I don't know how to be myself anymore.

In the next few weeks, even as the power remains steady, there is still a pall hanging over me. I wake up each morning expecting to find a limb missing. I plan for how I will make breakfast without my leg. I spend more time than usual in bed. Edgar says he wants his wife back.

"I wish I knew why this is happening," I reply. "Every day feels like the same day." Time has gotten away from me. But the situation is untenable. The outages keep happening.

"I've lost control of my body," I say. "I lost control when I got pregnant. I never got it back again."

He nods.

I venture out of the house during the next outage and see other women missing body parts. There are many of us. Hundreds, at least. This time, I've lost my leg again. Only women seem to be affected. They bag up groceries with one hand. They fill up their gas tanks while missing fingers. As the days go on, people gather in the streets in a rage. "*Give us back our limbs,*" we shout. I chat with a few hopping women. They have also been told their limbs are being stored in "the cloud." And what is with that customer-service menu, like they don't want us to get through? To whom are we supposed to complain? Is anyone listening? There isn't a news van in sight. I take comfort in the fact that I'm not alone. The utility company can't hide from us forever. The women assure me we will get answers.

One day at the bookstore, I meet a lady who is missing the visible part of her ears. I ask if she understands why we are being erased. She tells me there is an exposé coming out in the next few days. She has been in communication with the journalist, a friend from graduate school.

"Jaws will drop," she says.

The story comes out in the *Times*. Through the Freedom of Information Act, the journalist has gotten her hands on several illuminating documents from the Department of Missing Limbs, which is tasked with investigating the theft of body parts.

It turns out that while in "the cloud," our limbs are temporarily lent out to the victims of bombing campaigns abroad—some of the campaigns are secret, some not.

"It smells like a cover-up," my husband says.

I imagine that my leg supports a ten-year-old amputee who is about my height. My arm is lent to an orphan boy who needs my hand to grasp his medicine. I try to make sense of the image of a young child with a tired hand that should have been cutting up food into bite-sized toddler pieces, a hand that should have been pulling a fresh T-shirt over a small head. They only want the limbs of mothers. Now I see why. A soothing hand.

The idea is that there are enough limbs for everyone if we share—thanks to one young executive's idea of crowdsourcing. On paper, it sounds reasonable. Charitable even. War orphans deserve hands. If I weren't forced to participate, I would probably like the sound of this program. But then I realize if countries would quit bombing people, these amputees wouldn't need new hands.

We enter another heat wave. The governor asks us to be kind to our utility companies, to turn off our air-conditioning when it is hot—as if we didn't depend more on electricity in the historic heat.

My husband says he is desperate for life to go back to normal. He no longer sleeps at night. Sharing a bed with him is unbearable. He sleeps as close to the edge as possible. He won't cuddle with me when I am missing a limb. He says he is too afraid to occupy the space that should be occupied by my leg, like he is violating a law of physics. He says he needs to respect the space where my leg should be so that it will come back. Superstitions like these are keeping him sane. But what is keeping me sane? Who will hold me? I can't do this anymore. I don't have the strength.

He floats the idea of leaving California, but that would mean leaving behind our careers, our neighborhoods, and our friends. If only we could transport our life somewhere else. If only we had seen into the future and already built a life in that other place where the trees were never on fire and the power never went out. If only we didn't love the redwoods and the ocean and mountains. If only we hadn't grown attached to our bachelor mountain lion, who survived two freeway crossings while fleeing his inbred family so he could carve out a new life for himself in the park. He is no longer alive, but his spirit is still felt.

We start to do strange calculations to compare the value of friends to the value of clean air and electricity. Edgar points out that we never see our friends anymore, so why should they factor in? I tell him I'm still holding out hope that our social life will return when the smoke lifts.

I LOSE MY LIPS next. I hate not having lips. It's far worse than losing my arm. I can't speak clearly. It's like I don't exist. Ondine doesn't listen. She and Edgar have conversations that don't include me. When the lights come back, my lips are still gone. They must have gotten stuck across the transom.

"They'll come back soon," Edgar says. But I fear I'll never see them again.

One day in December it rains harder than I've seen, after ten years of drought. We get several years of precipitation in a few hours. The water seeps in through our roof. Cars float across the freeway. Houses slide into the ocean. Still, we rejoice in the change.

"I never thought the fires would stop," Edgar says.

"Twnoslftbun," I say, nodding. "Itsmazg."

"I know," he says. He's starting to understand me better.

I stand outside and get drenched by the rain. Drowning sounds like fun. I want to soak it in while it lasts. The rain will be gone soon. There is no way to capture it for the next drought. The water will spill into the ocean, as if the rain never happened.

After the storm passes, I reconnect with friends I haven't seen since I became a mother. Some of them are missing body parts too. I tell them I feel like I'm still living in a world where the lights are off. I follow up my words with texts to make sure I'm understood, but my friends know what I'm saying. They have similar thoughts. They have also become parents in an age of anxiety. They are angry about the inaction of politicians, outraged over what is happening to children abroad. Will our children live with a crushing weight, worse than ours? Will they have hope?

As the months pass, Ondine grows more independent. She is eager to have new experiences. I find a new joy in motherhood I had yet to discover: She is smart enough now to win arguments.

On her third birthday, she asks to see snow. Edgar and I haven't seen any in years. There is one mountain nearby that might have some. We drive six hours northeast to a cabin at eight thousand feet. The ground is mostly bare when we arrive. I can see that Ondine feels let down.

"Where's the snow?" she asks.

I tell her it's becoming more elusive these days—that you can no longer rely on seeing it, even in the middle of winter. It comes when it comes. At least in California.

"Why?" she asks. She has just started asking this question. We unpack the car and carry in the sled that we won't be using. I point out the beauty of the trees, the fresh air. There's plenty to love up here. But all she wants is snow. She isn't satisfied with the smell of clean air.

"Where did the snow go?" she asks again.

"Maybe if you go to sleep, the snow fairy will stop by," Edgar tells her. The forecast calls for a few inches overnight, though we can't be sure if it will stick around long enough for her to see it.

She falls asleep after repeating her question: "Where's the snow?"

In the morning, we wake up to over two feet of powder—far more than I expected. It's piled up against our window.

Edgar flings on his coat and runs outside, as if he fears the snow will be gone before he can get there. I dress Ondine and lead her outside.

"Is this real?" she asks.

"Yes," I tell her.

She runs out into the yard and shrieks with joy as her boots briefly disappear into the white.

ACKNOWLEDGMENTS

My literary agent, Martha Wydysh, who worked tirelessly on this collection. I can't thank you enough. Katy Nishimoto for editing with a keen eye and championing my stories. I'm so grateful to be working with you. Whitney Frick, Avideh Bashirrad, JP Woodham, Debbie Aroff, Corina Diez, Carrie Neill, Elizabeth Eno, Natasha Tsakiris, Michael Morris, and the entire team at Dial, who have been more supportive to a debut author than I could have imagined. Will Watkins at CAA. I feel lucky to be working with such a wonderful team.

Aram Mrjoian, Adam Dalva, and *Guernica,* Oscar Villalon at *Zyzzyva,* Anna Lena Phillips Bell and the team at *Ecotone,* Michael Nye and the team at *Story,* Wendy Lesser at *The Threepenny Review, Catapult, North American Review, Electric Literature, Southern Humanities Review, swamp pink, Gulf Coast, Chicago Quarterly Review.* I am deeply grateful to the literary journals that gave my stories their first homes. I would not have a collection today without these wonderful journals.

Steph Cha, Sarah LaBrie, Anne-Marie Kinney, and J. Ryan Stradal for the support, the late-night book discussions, and the life in and out of books. Thanks for being my community. Katya Apekina for the notes. Claire Dunnington for letting me know I had something worth pursuing when I first decided to write stories.

David MacDonald, Malinda McCollum, and Daniel Orozco, my teachers in the Stanford University creative-writing program; Brit Bennett, who mentored me at Tin House. I am also grateful to Lydia Kiesling, Kate Folk, MAB, Charlene Carruthers, Allison Carter, Torsa Ghosal, Meg Howrey, Julia Ingalls, Kristin Jones, Justin Lerner, Nina Mamikunian, Kate Osana Simonian, Anthony Veasna So, Chris Terry, Sara Finnerty Turgeon, and Annie Vitalsey.

The Simpsons for not giving me a writing job.

My parents, who taught me to love literature; my family, Ozzy, Harold, Maude, Isidore, Josh—this book would not exist without you.

PUBLICATION HISTORY

These stories were originally published as follows:

"I Am the Ghost Here"—*Guernica,* 2023
"Egg Mother"—*Catapult,* 2022
"Trash Heap Hero"—*The Threepenny Review,* 2024
"Return"—*North American Review,* 2024
"Muscle to Muscle, Toe to Toe"—*Zyzzyva,* 2025
"The Garbage Patch"—*Ecotone,* 2022

ABOUT THE AUTHOR

KIM SAMEK is a half-Thai Emmy-nominated writer and television producer who studied German literature and creative writing at Stanford University. Her stories have appeared in *Guernica, Ecotone, Electric Literature, North American Review, Chicago Quarterly Review, swamp pink, Gulf Coast, Southern Humanities Review, The Threepenny Review, Story,* and *Zyzzyva.* Her short fiction has won a Pushcart Prize and an O. Henry Award. A native of Seattle, she lives in Los Angeles.

kimsamek.com
Instagram: @the_kim_samek

ABOUT THE TYPE

This book was set in Sabon, a typeface designed by the well-known German typographer Jan Tschichold (1902–74). Sabon's design is based upon the original letter forms of sixteenth-century French type designer Claude Garamond and was created specifically to be used for three sources: foundry type for hand composition, Linotype, and Monotype. Tschichold named his typeface for the famous Frankfurt typefounder Jacques Sabon (c. 1520–80).